Exit 192

James A. Graves, Jr.

What others are saying about Exit 192:

Exit 192 is a wild ride that hooks readers as soon as Nick turns off the interstate at exit 192 and keeps you captivated until the book's end. It's a page turner filled with adventure, action, suspense, a touch of romance, and a look at technology, that you won't put down. Along with the fascinating read, it addresses the growing problem of human trafficking in this country. No matter what your favorite genre is, this one is for you. By Kathleen Walls author of The Casey Clark Realtor Mystery series and other books.

Exit 192 is a fast moving tale of love, secrets and the ugly side of human trafficking. After Nick takes an exit off of an interstate in West Texas and finds himself living a life that he never had, you'll find yourself pulling for Nick and Walela and their secret life.

As a writer, James keeps you interested with explicit details and plot turns that bring you into the story and keep you there until the dramatic end. I recommend Exit 192 highly for anyone that loves a good love story mixed with real time facts about the dangerous cartel world. By Beverly Gillis Author of Soul Journey

Exit 192 is primarily a historical fiction book, but with a touch of SCI-FI. There are surprising twists and a lot action. The book has an interesting story line, along with interesting characters. The primary character, Nick, is a man of integrity and he and his trusted friends will follow through until justice has been served. The villains of the story learned the hard way that you don't kidnap a family member or threaten the lives of loved ones and get away with it. Pay attention to the details as you read and you may see a hint of what's coming your way. You probably won't put the book down until you've finished. By Jerry from California

Much like his last great read, "The Wrong War", James has created an intriguing and unexpected plot to Exit 192. With plenty of action, a bit of romance, interesting and well-developed characters, and many unexpected moments in the story, James shows great imagination and the ability to put his imagination into words. Exit 192 is a fun and thought provoking read! By Erik from Bonifay, Florida

AKNOWLEDGEMENT

Jerry Sanchez
Thanks for your astute input, excellent editing, your friendship and gracious encouragement.

Erik Rice
Thanks for your enthusiasm for my novels, your friendship and unwavering support.

Nick, Walela and Tala
Thanks for allowing me to share your adventures.

OTHER BOOKS BY JAMES A. GRAVES, Jr.

Aftermath I: The Fight For Survival
Aftermath II: The Deadly Game
Assembly Line Justice: The American Drug War
Assembly Line Justice: How The American War On Drugs Has
Failed (2nd edition)
The Wrong War

The Author:

James A Graves, Jr.
Author, Songwriter, Musician, Pilot, Swamp Rat...
Leading a double-life as an electronics tech until he retired.
Born and raised in the Florida Panhandle. Spent his younger days in or around Morrison Spring, running the Choctawhatchee River, and as a guitarist/vocalist in a Rock Band.
Grew up escaping reality with 60's and 70's Rock & Soul, reading H.G. Wells, Isaac Asimov and watching Twilight Zone and The Outer Limits on TV.

Exit 192

by

James A. Graves, Jr.

ISBN: 979-8-9874547-1-8
Library of Congress Control Number: 2025903813
Published by Global Authors Publications

Filling the GAP in publishing

Interior Design by Kathleen Walls
Cover Design by Kathleen Walls
Cover Photo by James A. Graves, Jr.
Edited by Kathy Barnett

Déjà Vu

Nick awakened suddenly but didn't move. He didn't recognize his surroundings.

"Where am I?" he thought.

He had been having a most pleasant dream. It seemed almost real. As he glanced around the room he suddenly realized that it was his bedroom. But, still, somehow he wasn't sure it was where he was supposed to be. As he contemplated his situation, Walela moved slightly and he glanced down to find her cuddled against him. She was bathed in the half-light of early morning, sleeping peacefully and looking like an angel.

This had to be home. But it just didn't feel right. In the back of his mind Nick felt that he was supposed to be somewhere else. And in that life, he slept alone…

Follow the adventures of former Navy SEAL Nickolas Conner as he becomes entangled in a desperate and dangerous hunt for his wife's kidnapped sister while he tries to unravel the haunting flashbacks that suggest he should be living an entirely different life.

Table of Contents

Chapter 1 Home?

Nickolas Conner stared at the beautiful West Texas sunset bathing the desert sky in gold, crimson and sky-blue pink. Suddenly his daydreaming was rudely interrupted by the growl of the rumble strips on US Interstate Highway 10 as his Dodge Durango SRT Hellcat drifted onto the shoulder of the road.

"Crap! Pay attention, Nick," he said to himself with a bit of a Texas drawl as he steered back into the lane. Knowing that Texas State Troopers closely patrol the stretch of I-10 that runs through Van Horn, he added, "You're doin' eighty-five. The last thing you need is to be pulled over for reckless drivin'."

It was late summer of 2024, and after almost two months as the lead Civil Engineer overseeing a US Department of the Interior construction project near Redding, California, Nick was exhausted and tired of traveling. But yet, 15 hours of driving time still lay ahead before he would arrive at his home in Destin, Florida.

Nick looked at the radiant sunset once more and then scanned the horizon. Van Horn lay ahead in the distance. His fuel gauge showed just below half of a tank, so he decided that he would continue on to Fort Stockton, refuel there, and stay overnight at the Super 8 Motel where he had stayed many times before.

Crossing Texas never ceased to amaze Nick. It made up a full third of the trip from Redding to Destin. As he traveled through the Texas portion of the southwest desert, only a few miles north of the Mexico border, he looked at the rugged desolate country and felt as though he was on the surface of the moon, totally isolated from civilization.

Actually, quite a few folks made this part of Texas home. He would pass by cattle ranches and several small towns during the hour and a half or more before he reached Fort Stockton and his only overnight stay during the trip home.

Nick listened to music and watched the Texas desert scroll by at 85 miles per hour in the fading afternoon light. He was approaching the I-10/I-20 interchange. The left fork headed northeast toward Abilene and Dallas. Nick maintained 85 mph as he drifted over to the far-right lane and continued on I-10 east toward Houston, Pensacola and finally, home to Destin.

Suddenly Nick's mind was flooded with a strong sense that he was almost home. It was a shocking, overwhelming sensation at first, like the sudden realization of being lost due to a serious navigation error. But the shock was quickly replaced with a comforting, settling feeling of relief caused by the thoughts of "finally home" washing over him like a cool summer breeze.

In the scant space of a few minutes, Nick had gone from being 15 hours away from home to being less than 15 minutes from home.

Momentarily, he cancelled the cruise control and coasted down the off ramp of Exit 192. At the stop sign, he turned right and accelerated onto F.M. 3078 toward Toyahvale. His actions were automatic, as though he had taken this exit a hundred times.

Nick suddenly became a bit impatient, reached down and selected the "sport" mode of his supercharged hemi-powered Hellcat and opened it up. In seconds the powerful machine was doing 130 mph down the narrow two-lane asphalt farm road and rapidly accelerating.

The miles flew by and in minutes he pressed hard on the brake pedal, down-shifted the automatic transmission and turned left onto a gravel road that followed the winding path of a dry creek for just over a mile down a deep draw between low rolling hills.

Suddenly a little voice in the back of Nick's mind started screaming at him; "Warning! This is wrong. Stop! You should not be here. Think Nick, think!"

Moments later, as the faint, glowing light of dusk lit the western horizon and the first stars appeared, he swung happily onto the long driveway and parked underneath the carport of a quaint four-room log cabin.

Just as Nick opened the car door, a large and very excited golden lab came bounding from around the back of the cabin to greet him. Barking and tail wagging wildly, the dog put his front feet on Nick's chest, pushed him back into the seat and almost climbed into his lap.

"Hey Sprocket! Good to see you boy." Nick stroked Sprocket's fur and scratched behind his ears as the excited dog happily licked his face. "Yes, I missed you too pal."

Just then the side door swung open and a breathtakingly beautiful Cherokee Indian woman in her late twenties stepped out onto the porch. Walela (in the Cherokee language her name means Hummingbird) was barefoot, wearing a colorful beaded headband that helped keep her long, straight, silky dark hair flowing down her back. She wore cut-off jeans and an oversized white tee shirt tied in a knot at her waist, showing a bit of her bare belly. Walela loved dressing casual, especially around her home. Her simple outfit perfectly accentuated her petite five-foot, two-inch muscular frame and her sexy 34-22-34 inch figure.

She ran across the porch, down the steps and to the driver's side of the car, beaming a warm, loving smile.

"Welcome back, stranger! I was hoping that you would make it home before supper."

"Thanks," Nick replied, looking at her in total awe – in between the dog kisses. But he couldn't move. Sprocket had him pinned in the driver's seat.

"Alright Sprocket, down boy." Walela commanded, "You've given Nick enough welcome-home kisses. It's my turn." She took him by the collar, pulled him out of the car, petted him, and then whispered, "Fetch your ball."

Sprocket bolted away, heading for the back yard.

Nick stood up and Walela leaped into his arms, wrapped her legs around his waist and kissed him long and passionately. Then she hugged him tightly. Her physical strength surprised him.

"I have missed you, husband," she whispered in his ear and then kissed him again.

Nick stroked her silky hair that lay across her shoulders and halfway down her back and continued down until his hand rested on her firm bottom.

The feel of Walela's taught, bronze body against his made him reluctant to release his embrace and the sound of her soft, sexy voice was almost overwhelming. Nick instinctively knew that he was completely and totally hers and deep inside his soul, he felt that it had always been so.

But he was speechless. That was just as well, because he was not nearly done kissing her. In fact, at the moment, he never wanted to stop. However, a minute or so later, which seemed like a few seconds to Nick, Sprocket came trotting up with a bright orange squeaky ball in his mouth.

Just then Walela gasped, grabbed Nick's face with both hands and said, "Oh my! I have to stir the chili!"

She kissed him quickly and dashed away, running up the steps, across the porch, and through the open door.

Nick slumped back onto the driver's seat, looking somewhat dazed and whispered, "Wow!"

He heard a small squeak and looked down just as Sprocket dropped the ball. It squeaked again as it bounced and came to rest at Sprocket's front feet.

"I gather you wanna fetch?"

Sprocket quickly spun around, picked up the ball and squeaked it several times.

"Okay." Nick reached down and took the ball from Sprocket's mouth, stood up and pitched it far into the now-starlit back yard. Sprocket dashed away in pursuit. Nick reached into the back seat, retrieved his travel bag, and headed for the open door.

He walked through the door and into the large, ranch-style kitchen-dining room. It was filled with the fragrance of fresh-made tortillas and chili. Nick sat his bag down, shut the door, and walked across the kitchen to the stove. Walela was standing over a large steaming pot, stirring the contents.

Nick leaned over the pot and inhaled deeply. "Mmm! Your chili smells delicious! Did it get scorched while you were outside?"

"You tell me." She dipped the ladle into the pot, blew on it to cool it, and then handed it to Nick.

He tasted it and said, "Yum! That *is* delicious! And not scorched a bit."

Then he finished the contents of the ladle, laid it on the stove, took her into his arms and said, "But you're more delicious."

She smiled and giggled as he kissed her. Then he stroked Walela's beautiful face and her long black hair and continued, "You had me kind of twitter-pated out there with your delightful greeting. I didn't even say 'hello'."

Staring into her flashing green eyes, he said, "Hello. Hummingbird. You look so beautiful. I missed you, too."

And then he kissed her again, long and passionately.

Just then Sprocket blasted through the doggie door into the kitchen, trotted over to them and dropped his ball with a squeak.

"I think he missed you, too, husband," Walela observed.

They both looked down at Sprocket looking up at them and wagging his tail. Nick knelt down and petted him. Walela gave Sprocket the last bite of a tortilla she had been munching on.

"I don't worry as much about you being here alone because I know this guy is protectin' you," Nick commented. "I would actually feel sorry for anyone who tried to harm you. Their own mother probably wouldn't be able to recognize them after he was done."

"He's very protective. He stays right under my feet most of the time that you're gone."

Then she lifted the lid off the tortilla server, retrieved two tortillas, handed one to Nick, then tore the other in half, gave half to Sprocket and took a bite of her half.

"Ummm!" Nick exclaimed, "This is *so* good!"

"Thank you," she replied with a smile. Then said, "I am starving, let's eat!"

After supper, Nick helped Walela wash the dishes and clean up the kitchen. Then he poured them a glass of wine and they sat on the back porch, listening to the crickets singing and looking at the stars.

"That supper was delicious, Hummingbird. I'm so stuffed. I miss your cooking when I'm away. Almost as much as I miss you."

She turned to look at him and he winked at her.

Walela reached out and took his hand in hers. "You're sweet, my husband. I know you must travel, but I miss you terribly when you're away. I long for the day when you will no longer have to leave me."

"Me too, Hummingbird, me too," Nick replied wistfully, then asked, "Are you ready for bed? I'm exhausted. But first, I'm gonna take a shower."

"I'll wash these wine glasses and be there in a little bit," Walela replied, then she picked up the empty bottle and said, "Remind me to get more wine. We finished this one off."

"You mean *you* finished it off," Nick corrected her. "I only had two glasses."

Nick had been in the shower only a few minutes when Walela opened the shower door, dropped her robe to the floor and stepped in.

She smiled, kissed him and said, "You know how I hate to waste water…"

Chapter 2 Déjà Vu

Nick awakened suddenly, but didn't move. He didn't recognize his surroundings.

"Where am I?" he thought.

He had been having a most pleasant dream. It seemed almost real. As he glanced around the room, he suddenly realized that it was his bedroom. But, still, somehow he wasn't sure he was where he was supposed to be. As he contemplated his situation, Walela moved slightly and he glanced down to find her cuddled against him. She was bathed in the half-light of early morning, sleeping peacefully and looking like an angel.

"So it wasn't a dream..." He thought, and then whispered, "Wow! What's goin' on?"

He watched her as she slept. Her head rested on his left arm. Softly breathing. Her gorgeous body snuggled against him, her bare left leg across his legs.

"Man I'm glad I'm not dreaming!" he thought as he smiled and carefully brushed a long lock of hair from Walila's face.

She snuggled closer to him and faintly moaned. Memories of her flashed through his mind like lightning bolts from a distant thunderstorm. Confusing thoughts of the time before. She was waiting for him when he was deployed in Afghanistan. No. That was before he knew Walela. But he felt as though he had known her all of her life. As a child. Growing up. High school. College. Before the Navy SEALs. But the numbers didn't work. He had just turned 20. A sophomore at Annapolis. Walela was waiting for him back home. At 12 years old? The explosion. The fall of 2016. Wounded in action. An IED. His team. All dead. Severe traumatic brain injury. Surgery. Recovery at the Shephard Center in Atlanta. Walela was there. But she would have only been 19...

"How did this beautiful creature come to bless my life?" he asked himself silently. *"I know we belong together. But why me? What have I possibly ever done, or will ever do, to deserve her?"*

Nick slowly eased out of the bed, being very careful not to disturb Walela, kissed her ever so gently on her cheek, and tucked the covers around her. He quietly grabbed his pajama bottoms, crept from the bedroom, and closed the door. Then he went to the kitchen, put on his pajamas and a pot of coffee. When he finished, he walked out onto the back porch. Sprocket got up from his puppy pillow in the kitchen, yawned and stretched, then exited through the doggy door to join Nick on the porch.

"Good mornin', boy," Nick said as he kneeled down on one knee to pet Sprocket. The dog wagged his tail and looked up at him.

"Let's go check out the pond."

Sprocket jumped off the porch and trotted toward the pond. Nick walked down the steps and followed. Just as Sprocket reached the pond, several fish darted away from the water's edge and he sprinted into the water trying to catch one.

"Looks like the fish are a bit faster than you this mornin', Sprocket."

The dog stood still, belly-deep in the pond, intently watching for another fish. Nick sat down on the bench near the water's edge and took in the peaceful early morning scene. Within a fenced pasture near the pond, several cows, two horses. and a donkey grazed on lush green grass. The fenced area included a smaller pasture that was occupied by a large, solitary bull named "Attitude.". The fence continued on to a corral and a large barn located several hundred feet behind the cabin.

The sun's rays silently peaked over the top of a mesa in the distance. Water bubbled from a tall outcropping of stones and boulders across the pond from where he sat. The sound of the waterfall created a restful ambiance.

Nick felt as though he had repeated this morning routine with Sprocket countless times. He loved the sound of the waterfall. But, quite mysteriously, he also felt as though he was somehow experiencing all of this for the first time. Yet, he fondly remembered skinny dipping in the pond with Walela many times.

He contemplated his confusing memories for a few minutes. Then he suddenly stood up, dropped his pajama bottoms, waded into the pond up to his waist and dove in. Nick was an easy-going, 35-year-old athlete of Scottish descent, with short-cropped brown hair and blue-eyes. He had the lean, muscular body of a quarterback, packed into a two hundred pound, six-foot frame.

The cool water felt refreshing. Sprocket followed, swimming right behind him, trying to keep up. Nick rolled over onto his back, swimming much slower and allowing Sprocket to catch up. They swam the remaining distance across the pond together.

Nick stopped near the waterfall, found his footing on the slick, rocky bottom and carefully stood up underneath the icy, spring-fed waterfall. It flowed from a rocky ledge about ten feet above him. Standing chest deep in the pond, Nick looked up and let the cold water splash his face, then he caught some water in his cupped hands and drank. The water, flowing from an artesian spring and bubbling up from a large aquifer system that also fed other artesian springs in the area including San Solomon Spring, was sweet and delicious.

Sprocket swam in a circle around him and then went to the pond's edge, climbed up on the rocky bank and shook the water off of his fur. Suddenly Nick dove in again, swimming underwater. Sprocket jumped in and followed him. Nick surfaced several hundred feet away near the edge of the pond, retrieved his pajama bottoms, and headed toward the back porch with Sprocket right on his heels.

Nick looked at Sprocket, "That was fun! Huh, boy?"

Sprocket sprinted away, made a fast circle of the yard and then flopped down on his back to wallow in the lush green lawn.

Nick went to the coffee pot, poured two cups, stirred in some extra ingredients, walked to the bedroom and silently sat the cups down. He carefully lifted the covers off of the still-sleeping Walela, crept onto the bed and laid on top of her.

She woke with a gasp and squealed, "Eeeeekk! What are you doing? You're freezing ...and wet!"

Just then, Sprocket came into the room. He had just taken another dip in the pond and was dripping wet. He jumped on the bed and began wallowing on top of them.

"Noooo!!" Walela screamed. "Get off my bed you wet mongrels!"

Sprocket continued wallowing on Walela as Nick laughed.

"Mongrels!" She yelled again.

"Mongrels?"

"Yes! Plural! You're a couple of wet mongrels!"

She pushed Sprocket away, sat up and pointed at Nick, "You! Get off my bed and get me a towel!"

Then she pointed at Sprocket, "And you! Just *get*!"

Sprocket jumped from the bed and bolted out of the room into the kitchen, then continued through the doggy door to the outside. Nick returned with a towel and handed it to Walela.

"Dry your hair first," She ordered. "You're still dripping, too."

"I don't believe you two!" She complained.

"I was sleeping sooo comfortably." She pouted pitifully and fell back on her pillow.

"I brought you coffee…" Nick offered with an apologetic tone.

"Give me the towel first. I'm soaked." Then she raised her voice again, "That dog was soaking wet!"

"Now that wasn't my idea," Nick explained, trying to throw Sprocket under the bus. Walela dried herself as she listened.

"He was wallowing on the lawn when I came in to get your coffee. He must've went for another swim. I didn't call 'im or anything."

Nick couldn't hold it in any longer and burst out laughing.

"You *did* set that up!" Walela growled, "You, you…"

She quickly swung the towel over his head, yanked him onto the bed, and tackled him. After they wrestled for a bit, she pinned him on the bed with her knees on his shoulders and her hands holding his wrists, pinning his arms over his head.

"Nickolas Conner, you and that dog are going to pay for this," she growled down at him.

"Oh? And how exactly are we going to pay, Miss Hummingbird?"

She looked pensive and replied calmly, "I haven't decided yet. But you *will* pay…"

Just then Nick rolled quickly, sending Walela onto her back on the bed. He pinned both of her arms over her head and kissed her long and hard. She fought his advances for a moment, then relinquished and returned his kiss with much passion.

They stopped kissing for only a moment as she said, "Well, your punishment will have to wait…" then she wrapped her arms around his neck and pulled him to her.

Sometime later they were lying face-to-face, staring into each other's eyes.

She kissed him softly and said, "I love you, husband."

"I love you too, Hummingbird."

"I have no fear when I am with you." Walela's voice was soft and gentle. "I feel complete and content. I've never known emotions like this. No man has ever made me feel…" She searched for the right words. "As one… as though we are one. Does that make sense?"

"Yes. I complete you, and make you feel whole."

"Yes. That is how I feel."

"You make me feel the same way," Nick confessed. "When I look at you. When we kiss. When we make love. I feel as though we have always been together and were meant to be together. As though we are on the path that God intended for us to travel. As mates. As one."

He pulled her on top of him and they kissed again, tenderly. Then Walela laid her head on his chest and sighed deeply.

"But you're troubled." Nick sensed.

"Yes," she confessed.

"Can you tell me why?"

"I fear the future."

"Why fear the future? That is in God's hands."

"I see dark clouds ahead."

Nick held her close, stroked her hair and they fell asleep.

Later that morning, Walela was still sleeping in Nick's arms. She stirred, opened her eyes, yawned and stretched. Nick felt her move and massaged her back from her shoulders to her bottom with both hands as she stretched.

"Mmmmm, that feels soooo good," she purred.

"I totally agree." Nick smiled as he lifted her face to his and kissed her.

"Good morning, Hummingbird."

"Good morning, husband. What time is it?"

"Just after ten."

"Oh my! I haven't slept this late in forever."

"Well, I, for one, am glad you did," he admitted as he stroked her hair with his right hand and caressed her bare bottom with his left.

She smiled, kissed him tenderly, and laid her head on his chest.

Just then, Sprocket, who was stretched out on the foot of the bed, wagged his tale.

"Good morning, Sprocket," Walela said in a droll tone.

Sprocket wagged his tail faster, sounding like a drum as his tail thumped the mattress.

"He's still wet," Walela lamented as she rubbed his belly with her foot.

"Sprocket, we need to have a discussion about swimming and then getting on my bed."

Sprocket raised his head and licked her foot.

"I love you, too," Walela sighed.

Nick looked at the coffee cups on the night stand and said, "Our coffee got cold. I need to make another pot."

"You're sweet," Walela said. "Let's go for lunch instead. I'm starving."

Nick got out of bed and began getting dressed. Walela crawled to the foot of the bed, looked down at Sprocket and said, "I would get dressed, but I have to take a shower because I *smell like a dog!"*

Sprocket lifted his head and licked her face, wagging his tail wildly. He and Walela were almost nose to nose as she sternly ordered, "Get off my bed."

He licked her face again and rolled onto his back, trying to look cute and defuse her annoyance by appearing vulnerable. It didn't work.

"Go!" She growled.

Sprocket scrambled off the bed and bolted out the door.

Nick watched the scene, both amused by Sprocket's antics and very much enjoying watching Walela crawl around on the bed naked. He walked to the bed, reached out and pulled her to the edge. She was on her knees. He wrapped his arms around her, pulled her to him and kissed her.

Then, looking down to conceal her smile, Walela simply asked, "Twitter-pated?"

"Yep," he replied, "Totally twitter-pated."

She looked up at him with loving, innocent eyes and said, "If we start something now we'll never make it to lunch."

He lifted her backwards to the middle of the bed, supported her head with his hand, gently laid her onto the bed and made passionate love to her.

Chapter 3 Déjà Vu Again

The early afternoon was sunny and peaceful. A blue quail, perched atop a mesquite tree, sang his call announcing his territory to all within hearing. A cactus wren, chasing a bug, darted through the jasmine hedge by the bedroom window as a cooling breeze gently moved the curtains and swayed the trees beside the pond. From the peak of the roof, a mocking bird proudly sang her long list of borrowed bird calls.

Nick and Walela lay in each other's arms, holding hands and quietly listening to the world go by.

"I can't remember when we've spent most of the day in bed," Walela commented.

"Me either," Nick replied, "But I could sure get used to this."

"Me too," she replied as she brought his hand up to her lips, kissed it and then pressed his palm against her face.

Then she continued, changing the subject to food, "A few hours ago I said I was starving, now I'm downright famished."

"I could eat, too," Nick agreed, then said, "I'm gonna take a quick shower and then call the boss. I still have to upload my trip report. I intended to do that last night after I stopped in…"

Nick's voice trailed off.

"When you stopped where last night?" Walela asked.

"I'm… not… sure. I think I was about to say Fort Stockton."

"You were planning to go to Fort Stockton last night?"

"No, I was anxious to get home to you. I'm not sure why that popped in my head. But I feel like I've stopped overnight in Fort Stockton many times before."

Nick paused and looked at the floor, trying to remember, then looked at Walela. "Anyway… I'll take care of all that while you shower and get ready. Then we'll go eat and have a few drinks, too."

Nick finished everything he had to do and was walking into the bedroom just as Walela was putting on her shoes. Nick wore jeans, a western-style long-sleeve shirt, roper boots, and a tan cowboy hat. Walela wore a lovely knee-length, sleeveless yellow-print dress, leather sandals, and a Cherokee-designed headband.

"Wow!" Nick commented, "You are beautiful!"

"Thank you." She smiled humbly and blushed.

"Are you ready?" He asked.

"Yes. And if we don't find food pretty soon, I'm going to be out in the pasture grazing with the cattle."

"Yes ma'am!" Nick chuckled, then suggested, "Let's take your Raptor."

"Okay," She agreed.

Just as they stepped outside, Nick remembered something.

"Oh! I almost forgot, I have a gift for you."

"Awww! How sweet!"

Nick walked toward his Durango and just as he got even with the front bumper, he stopped abruptly, hesitated a moment, then stepped back and leaned over to look at the front license plate.

Walela noticed his odd actions and asked, "Did you find a ding from a rock or something?"

"No…" Nick replied, sounding distracted.

"Then what?" she insisted.

"I have a front tag," he replied, as if he had discovered something new.

"And?"

Nick just looked at her quizzically.

"Well?" she persisted.

"Well what?"

"You said you have a front tag. So does my truck. Everybody has one. Why are you acting as though you have just discovered your front license plate?"

Nick looked at the bumper again, kneeled down, took off his hat, scratched his head, and replied, "I'm not sure. It's just, for an instant, I was thinkin' that I shouldn't have a front tag because they're not required. Florida does not require front licenses plates, Nick was thinking. But why was I thinking about Florida?

That little voice in the back of Nick's mind was screaming at him again, julst like it did during his trip home, after he took Exit 192; "Warning, Nick! Something isn't right here. This should not be happening. Stop and think." Nick paused and stared at the Texas tag. Something was wrong; he just couldn't place it.

"They've always been required in Texas," Walela stated, sounding a bit annoyed. "You know that."

"Yeah, you're right…"

He looked at Walela again, then looked down at the bumper once more as he stood up. He went to the back of the Durango, opened the deck lid, retrieved a fairly large package, and brought it to her.

She took it from him and exclaimed, "On my! What is it?"

"Open it. Here, let me hold it for you."

She opened the box and found a beautiful coiled basket, woven with an intricate American Indian-style pattern.

"Nick it is amazing!" she gasped. "I just love it!"

She stood on her tiptoes, hugged his neck, and kissed him.

"You are so sweet! Thank you, my husband! Where did you find it?"

"It's made by the Maidu Tribe of Northern California. I know how you like to collect baskets from your tribe and others. So when I saw it, I knew you'd love it."

"Yes! It's perfect! You go start the truck, I'll just put this in the house and be right there."

The black Ford F-150 Raptor rumbled as Nick opened the passenger door and helped Walela climb up into the truck.

"Buckle up," he warned.

"You have a lead foot," she complained as he closed her door.

"I know," he replied as he buckled his seatbelt and gunned the powerful machine down the driveway toward the paved road.

As Nick turned left onto F.M. 3078, heading in the direction of Toyahvale and Balmorhea, he glanced at Walela sitting beside him and said, "Hang on." Then he stomped the accelerator.

The Raptor jumped to the right as all four tires spun, trying to find traction and boiling smoke from the burning rubber. He steered the truck straight as it regained traction and quickly pushed the speedometer past 100 mph.

"You're hopeless," she lamented. "The speed limit is 75, not 105." Then she added, "And you're wearing out my tires!"

"I know. But it's so much fun!" He grinned mischievously, then reassured her, "Don't worry, I'll buy you more tires. I think this thing needs more aggressive off-road tires anyway."

"I hear those things grow on trees out here somewhere," she replied sarcastically.

"I wish. I know tires are expensive, but we can afford it. I have a fat per diem check coming from my trip expenses. Besides, it'll give us a chance to run up to Pecos, maybe catch a movie, and go to dinner."

"That sounds nice," she replied, sounding a bit more positive.

Presently, they passed through Toyahvale and past the Balmorhea State Park, the home of San Solomon Spring. As he reached Balmorhea, Nick cruised slowly through town, then continued on to the interstate and took the frontage road eastward which led them to the Circle Bar & Saddleback Steakhouse near I-10 exit 212.

It was late Friday afternoon and the place was busy. Other cars and trucks were pulling in as Nick pulled up to the front door and said, "You go ahead and get us a table while I park."

"That works. See you inside," Walela replied, climbed out of the truck and walked in the front door.

The hostess greeted her as she walked in and asked, "How many in your party?"

Walela replied, "Two."

"We're clearing a table right now. It will only be a few minutes," the hostess replied with a smile.

"Thank you," Walela said.

Just then, a young guy who was leaning on a pool cue beside the pool table nearest the front door, dressed like a fancy cowboy and holding an almost-empty beer mug, whistled rudely at Walela. He was wearing a tight black tee shirt, blue jeans and a belt with a large silver buckle, cowboy boots with silver trim, and a black felt cowboy hat with feathers.

He spoke out in a loud voice, "Well, well, what do we have here? I've found myself a pretty little squaw. And she's all alone."

Walela ignored him. The hostess leaned close to her and said, "Be careful. He's drunk. He's been drinking for several hours."

"Thanks. No problem," Walela replied.

Then the guy walked up to her and said, "Hey, Pocahontas. Let me buy you a beer. Oh, wait! Let me check." Then he looked at the hostess and asked, "Do y'all serve Indians? I want to buy this cute little squaw a beer."

Just then, Nick came in the door, looked at Walela and asked, "How long is the wait?"

The guy looked at Nick and said, "Hey dude, you get your own. This is my squaw."

Nick walked over to the hostess and asked, "How long is the wait?"

"How many in your party?"

"Two," Nick replied, "I'm with the squaw."

The hostess gave him a look so dirty that it could've stained a napkin, then looked at the drunk guy and said, "Sir, you're annoying this lady. Please take a seat at the bar, there's plenty of room."

"I'll sit down if my squaw will come with me," he replied.

Then the hostess turned back to Nick and whispered, "Aren't you going to do something? That man is insulting your wife!"

Nick looked at Walela and asked, "How you doing, Hummingbird?"

She winked at Nick and said, "No problem."

The hostess looked at Nick quizzically, opened her mouth to speak, but then thought better of it. Nick suddenly recalled another scene in California when Walela handled an obnoxious drunk. He leaned closer to the hostess and whispered, "Somethin' tells me this ain't her first rodeo."

Just then Walela turned and spoke to the drunk, "Cowboy, you really should listen to the hostess."

"Aw to hell with this shit!" the drunk announced, then grabbed Walela by the left arm and said, "Come on squaw, let's go get drunk and have some fun."

As he tried to pull her with him, she swung in front of him and landed a blow with the butt of her right hand directly to his solar plexus. The drunk immediately lost his grip on her arm as both of his arms went limp and dropped to his side. He hunched over, then slowly sank to his knees.

As he knelt there, gasping and coughing, Walela lifted his hat, patted him on the head and said, "Cowboy, you have a loud mouth."

Then she replaced his hat, looked at the hostess, and asked, "Is our table ready?"

The hostess just stared at the drunk in amazement and then smiled at Walela and said, "That was amazing!"

Suddenly applause erupted from several ladies that had been watching the scene.

Nick just looked at the hostess and smiled.

The hostess gave Nick a sideways glance, then looked at Walela, "Yes ma'am, your table is ready now. This way please."

She waited for Walela, paused, leaned close, and whispered, "Honey, that was amazing! You have *got* to show me how to do that!"

"Just a solid hit with the butt of your hand to the solar plexus," Walela replied, "I practiced on my brothers."

Nick took Walela's hand and kissed it, then said, "That was cool, Hummingbird. I'll be right with you after I revive your victim."

She winked at Nick and followed the hostess.

Nick walked over to the drunk, reached down and helped him stand up.

"Just breathe kid, you'll live. Let's walk it off."

Nick guided him toward the bar and helped him sit down on a bar stool. Then he flagged the bartender and asked, "Ma'am, can we have a couple bottles of Lone Star?"

"Sure thing," she replied.

Nick looked at the drunk and asked, "How you doin', cowboy?"

"I ain't sure," he replied weakly.

The bartender brought their beers.

"Thanks," Nick said and handed her a ten dollar bill, took a sip, then looked at the drunk, and said, "My lady awaits."

As Nick started to stand up, the drunk blurted out, "Why did she hit me? I was just havin' a little fun."

Hearing the drunk guy's comment, the bartender stood close by and listened.

"Unfortunately, you were havin' a *little fun* at my wife's expense. You not only insulted her race and her heritage, but you also treated her like she was some cheap hooker."

"So why didn't you step up? Ain't you her husband?"

"If I had my way, I would've taken your sorry ass out in the desert, slit your throat and watched you bleed to death. Then buried your body and you'd never be heard from again. But I wasn't about to embarrass my wife. She didn't need my help. After all, she was just playin'. She saw that you were drunk. She had no intention of taking advantage of you. She's a genuinely good person. *I'm* not."

"Playin'!? She almost knocked me out! Took all I could do to keep from throwin' up."

"Look, she grew up with four older brothers. Mean brothers. All four have scars, physical scars, given to them because they occasionally made her mad during their many fights. Cowboy, you need to count your blessings. If you *had* made her mad, she would've taken you outside and kicked your sorry ass. And, one more thing, if you as much as look at my wife crossways from this moment on, I'll have *my* way. I *will* kill you."

Nick took his beer and went to have dinner with his Hummingbird.

The bartender watched Nick walk away and commented, "I like him!"

On the drive home after dinner, Nick silently drove normal.

"I hope that scene did not upset you," Walela commented.

"No sweetheart. That was awesome. I'm proud of you. One thing for certain, that cowboy won't bother you again."

"Did you really threaten to kill him?"

"It wasn't a threat."

"You would actually kill the guy for looking at me again?"

"I meant what I said."

"That scares me, Nick. I don't like to think of you as someone who would indiscriminately kill another human being. You speak of killing like it's an easy thing."

"It wouldn't be indiscriminate."

"So, he looks at me. Does he deserve to be murdered for that?"

"It's the principle of the thing. What he did was wrong in so many ways and on so many levels. I've seen that kind of animal too much. It was a shock to me to learn that so many of those guys exist. In high school, tryin' to take advantage of a girl that didn't want to be treated that way. Girls and women raped and abused by enemy soldiers. Even by coalition soldiers.

"I caught one of the contract security guards raping a 13-year-old Afghan girl and almost beat the bastard to death. She stayed to watch, so I decided to let her make the choice. I tied him to a post, gave her his knife, and walked away. I went back and the guard's throat had been cut. I heard later that one of the other guards supposedly did it.

"I made certain that she got proper medical attention. Just as I was about to leave, she hugged me and not a little girl hug, but a mature woman hug. She looked into my eyes – I'll never forget. She was beautiful. Her skin was dark golden brown and her eyes were sky-blue-gray. Then she handed me the knife wrapped in a cloth. It still had blood on it."

"All the terrible things that you have seen. The violence, killing and other atrocities, has had a profound effect on you. I'm afraid that you have become so accustomed to killing and death that it has become meaningless to you."

"My psychologist at Sheppard Center was concerned about that, too. She counselled me one-on-one, and in group sessions as well. After almost a year, she finally realized that we're considered lethal weapons for a reason – we're trained to kill when necessary. We don't kill because we like to kill, we kill when we have no other option."

"But that drunk cowboy didn't deserve to be killed. Certainly not to have his throat cut. He meant no harm."

"Are you kiddin' me? He'd rape you and not think a thing about it. In fact, he'd brag to his buddies about it and then rape you again the first chance he got. And he's no cowboy. My grandpa was a cowboy. That's an honorable profession. The jerk that insulted you is just a drunk. And alcohol just makes him more vulgar."

"Maybe you're right. I just don't want to believe it."

"That's because you're a truly good person."

Walela thought about what she was doing to Nick and replied, "I could disagree. But I'm worried about you. You seem angry. Something else is bothering you. I can tell when you're troubled. Besides, you are driving like an old man."

Nick gave Walela a surprised glance. "Well, it's these strange déjà vu things that's been happening to me. Like Fort Stockton. And the deal with my license plate. And the pond."

"What about the pond?"

"I was sittin' on the bench this morning before Sprocket and I went for a swim and I suddenly felt like it was the first time I'd ever seen the pond and the waterfall in daylight. I mean, I know that I saw it last night when we were sittin' on the back porch. But, I also know that I love to sit on the bench in the early mornin' and listen to the waterfall. And I remember us skinny dippin' many times. I just don't get it. Am I goin' nuts?"

Walela reached out and caressed his shoulder. "You are not going nuts, my sweet husband. You have just been working too hard. You are exhausted. You should call your boss and request a couple of week's leave. You have been so involved in all of those projects. We have not taken any leave in almost a year. We could go to Galveston and play on the beach. Or maybe go to the mountains. Just some time away from work will do you a world of good."

"Maybe you're right," Nick agreed, "Takin' leave is a good idea. I'm sorry I've been so involved with work."

"You don't need to apologize, sweet man. You are dedicated. It is your job to provide for me and I am very proud that you do that so well. My grandmother would say that you are a great hunter because you always keep my pots full of fresh meat."

"Thanks, Hummingbird. And I like your grandmother's thinkin'."

Chapter 4 The Next Step

Nick and Walela had discussed it and decided to spend their vacation playing on the beaches of South Texas. While she finished packing, Nick had gone into town to buy a few things for the trip. When he returned, he found Walela on the back porch sitting on the glider. She had a wine glass in her hand and a half-full bottle of wine beside her.

Nick sat down and said, "I got the stuff. You takin' a break?"

She didn't answer.

"What's wrong, Hummingbird? You okay?"

She lifted the glass to her lips but Nick took it before she could take another drink and sat the glass and the bottle aside.

"You've had enough," Nick said.

"Mom just called. Today is Tala's 16th birthday. I had forgotten. She's been missing for more than six months. I don't think mom can take much more. There is hardly ever any good news. Just vague reports of Tala being seen someplace. But when the cops go there, no one knows anything. Mom is a strong and brave lady, but she is not going to be able to handle this much longer."

Walela looked at Nick and said, "I am afraid the stress is going to kill her!" and fell into his arms crying.

Nick held and comforted her for a while, then tried to reassure her. "The FBI is pretty good at finding kidnapped kids. I'm sure they'll find her soon."

She raised her face and looked at Nick. "Husband, you know just as well as I do that they consider Tala just another wild teenage runaway Indian girl. She disappeared from a party with under-age drinking. They initially said that she was drunk and ran off with some older guy. If she was the daughter of a rich white family they would be searching everywhere. But Tala does not matter to them."

Walela sat up, then wiped the tears from her eyes and looked at the floor. "I have made a decision."

"What do you mean?" Nick asked.

"I am sorry," Walela replied. "I know we were planning to go to the beach, but I am going to search for Tala."

"How are you planning to do that?"

"In high school and college, I worked as an intern with the Cherokee Nation Marshal Service. After college, I hired on with the Bureau of Indian Affairs. I did a lot of undercover work on our reservation and others. The cartels were moving into some of the reservations, setting up business selling alcohol, drugs, and prostitution. I hated it.

"After Tala disappeared on that school trip to Dallas, I left BIA and began trying to find out what was being done to find her. My father works for the Cherokee Nation Health Services. My mother is a housewife, so they could not afford to hire an investigator. When I learned that very little was being done, I tried to find someone or some organization that would help search for my sister. Finally, I met a member of the Texas Rangers Human Trafficking Unit. I learned that they were serious about stopping human trafficking and had rescued a lot of people, mostly young girls being sex trafficked. But I just felt like I needed to do something. And now I have decided that I *will* do something.

"I've been talking to Seth Buxton, a lieutenant with the Texas Rangers Human Trafficking Unit in Austin. Because of my previous law enforcement training, he was willing to meet with me for an interview. At our next meeting, I am going to volunteer as an undercover resource. That way I can infiltrate those animals, gather intelligence and maybe help find Tala."

"Do you realize what you're sayin'?" Nick replied in alarm. "That's just the wine talkin'. The Cartels are nothing but a vicious, heartless bunch of animals. For God sake, Walela, they rape babies! They torture and kill for fun. Even if you do successfully infiltrate that snake pit, you'll be raped and abused just to initiate you into the life of being a sex slave. And if they even suspect that you're a spy, they'll torture you until they find out who you work for and then gang rape you to death! If they learn that you're working for Los Diablos Tejanos (translation: The Texan Devils – the nickname given to the Texas Rangers by the cartels) God only knows what horrible things they'll do to you before they kill you!"

"How is it that you know so much about these Cartel animals?" She asked.

"I can read!" Nick replied sarcastically, then quickly backtracked.

He reached out and hugged her. "I'm sorry, Hummingbird. I'm just shocked and upset that you would consider somethin' like this."

"I understand, my sweet love. You have every right to feel that way. But seriously, how *do* you know so much about them?"

"I have a fellow SEAL that's an FBI agent. We keep in touch. He's part of the human trafficking taskforce. His job is to track down missing persons. He's told me as much as he can about it. He says the cartels that run the slave trade are as bad, or worse, than the Muslim terrorist organizations. They also consider women property, use them sexually, abuse them and treat them like animals. The thing is, people who try to rescue their daughters usually also end up missing, or found dead, and used to send a message to other families who might try it.

"One thing for certain, you're not going undercover into the sewer that is the lair of those animals. And if you do get involved, at any level, I'm goin' with you."

"Now I must ask *you*, husband, do you realize what *you're* saying?"

"Yes."

"What about your job?"

"I'll have to take a leave of absence. That shouldn't be a problem."

"What will we do for income?"

"I was in rehab for over two years after I was wounded. I was diagnosed as incapable of managing my affairs. My parents were given power of attorney. They assumed the job of managing my Navy income and my retirement portfolio. Apparently it took quite a bit of financial maneuvering, but dad was able to invest most of my pay into my retirement fund - Thrift Savings Plan. When I finally recovered and got my life back, I resigned my commission, rolled my funds out of the government's control and into a really aggressive wealth management account and just let it continue to grow. I checked my account not long ago and it shows that I have almost two million dollars."

"Oh my! I had no idea."

"I'm sorry. I don't know why I haven't told you. I don't believe in keeping secrets from you. You're my wife. We're partners. We shouldn't keep anything from each other."

"Thank you for being honest with me." Walela hugged him. "And thank you for being willing to help me find Tala."

Her mind was racing. The flood of emotions were almost unbearable. She felt a wave of relief and joy that she would finally be able to search for her sister, coupled with profound thankfulness that Nick was willing to risk his life to help her. But those feelings were being drenched with the shame that she felt for having tricked and deceived him in order to make this moment happen.

There was a knot in the pit of her stomach and a wave of nausea swept through her. She had not anticipated that Nick would be so honest and noble. He just said that he would kill for her. She expected that he would feel sorry for her, be empathetic toward her grief and worry about Tala, and feel compelled to help with her search. This man was nothing like she thought he would be. Nick was a fierce and brave warrior. And he obviously loved her.

She remembered sitting by the fireplace on cold winter nights as a child with her mother and sister, listening to her grandmother tell tales of great tribal chiefs and fierce warriors who fought gallantly for her tribe. Honorable men who were kind and loving husbands, always faithful to their wives, and great hunters who always kept their cooking pots full of meat. Those men were devoted protectors who placed the safety of their wife and family, as well as their tribe, above all else.

But Walela had never witnessed that kind of man personally. Her father was a good man whom she looked up to. She was proud of him and the men in her family, but they were not like Nick. He was different. He stirred something deep within her.

Around her she saw many turbulent and broken homes and families, mostly due to alcohol and drug abuse. Divorce and infidelity were more common than happy marriages and close families. Walela had told herself that her grandmother's stories were nothing more than wishful tales to romanticize the past. She held no hope that she would ever find a husband who portrayed the virtues of the great warriors in her grandmother's stories. A man like that was, to Walela, a myth. Yet here he was, holding her in his strong arms.

And she was falling deeply in love with him. But everything that Nick knew of their relationship, of their life and their story, was a lie. A total fabrication of her making. Walela hated herself at that moment. She felt as though she no longer had honor. And what haunted her most was the thought of what her grandmother would think of her now…

Chapter 5 Walela's Quandary

Early one morning, just after sunrise, Walela drove to Calera Chapel, a small, historic landmark church near Toyahvale. She kneeled at the altar and prayed to God for Tala's safety and for His protection and guidance as they endeavored to find and rescue her kidnapped sister.

In the days that followed, Walela flew from Waco to Tulsa, Oklahoma and then drove to Muskogee where her parents lived. She had arranged to bring her mother to stay at the cabin to take care of Sprocket and the livestock.

After they returned, Nick and Walela met with Lieutenant Seth Buxton at the Texas Ranger Company "F" outpost in Waco. After his discussions with Walela, and as a result of her pleading, the lieutenant had compiled a digital file of the investigation into Tala's disappearance.

Several days later, after reviewing the file, they arranged another meeting…

"So, now that you've had time to review the file, what do you think?" Lieutenant Buxton asked.

"There's not much there," Walela commented. "Not many leads."

"That's probably the most frustrating thing about this job. I've been with the Human Trafficking Unit for five years. After a while some of the cases really get to you. We're required to rotate cases periodically. That hopefully heads off the tendency of a Ranger to become obsessed with any particular case. There are a surprising number of suicides in the Human Trafficking Enforcement community nationwide."

"I have never considered the search for Tala from your perspective. I am afraid that I had very low expectations of what law enforcement would do to find my sister. I am sorry."

"You have every reason to feel that way," Lieutenant Buxton reassured her. "I know the history of the American Indian's fight for equality. My wife is Apache."

"Will you be able to provide any support if and when we need it?" Nick asked.

"I'm sorry, but no, I won't," Lt. Buxton replied. "I'll get my ass in a fix if my superiors find out I've provided y'all with a copy of Tala's file. Missus Conner, I believe that you're qualified to do some of the intelligence gathering missions that we need to help stop human trafficking, but we cannot encourage or endorse the involvement of civilians, especially families who are emotionally involved.

"But don't misunderstand, we're all emotionally involved. By that, I mean The Rangers. A year ago we lost Ranger Lisa Blake, one of the bravest people I've ever known. She volunteered to allow herself to be kidnapped, enabling her to infiltrate that rat's nest and find out as much as possible about the organizations behind human trafficking along the border."

"Was Ranger Blake able to provide any intel?" Nick asked.

"Not much. She was killed before she was able to complete her mission. But I believe it was the Serpiente Cartel. The Snake," Lt. Buxton revealed. "A paid informant, Luis Soto, a traitor, sold her out. When they learned that she worked for Los Diablos Tejanos, every soldier of the Serpiente raped her. 130 men. It went on for three days. Somehow she managed to survive it. Then they tied her hands to a rope hanging from the ceiling and took turns whipping her with their belts until she died. Finally, they dragged her behind a vehicle through a town just south of the border, then out into the desert and left her body for the animals."

"Oh my God," Walela whispered as she wiped tears from her eyes.

"We know this," Lt. Buxton continued, "because they videoed all of it and then hand-delivered the video to our company headquarters here in Waco. The Serpiente didn't autograph it, but a guy just walked in, laid it on the security screener's desk and walked out. And that's their style, arrogant and fearless."

Nick looked at Walela. He knew what they were up against. She looked at him with fear and doubt in her eyes. But the lieutenant had more to say.

"The data that I gave you doesn't mention the Serpiente Cartel. We couldn't find enough hard evidence to legally tie them to drug trafficking, human trafficking, prostitution, murder, or anything else. A lot of coyotes and other small, non-affiliated operators feed the snake and they take all the heat. But they don't talk. They know what would happen.

"Soto claimed to have connections to Serpiente. But he played us. I think he was acting as a double agent. I made it my mission to find Soto. Unfortunately, I found him dead. They cut his throat and carved their logo into his chest. And that, more than any other evidence, convinced me Serpiente was responsible. Due to their arrogance, they just couldn't resist sending the message. I found it strange that they would execute him in such a public way considering that he put them onto a Los Diablos Tejanos spy. Apparently Serpiente doesn't even trust their own informants. It also shows that they won't hesitate to kill their own to protect the snake."

"I appreciate your blunt honesty, Lieutenant," Nick said.

"I just felt that you needed to know. Missus Conner, I know that you're determined to find your sister. And Lieutenant Commander Conner, I know that, as a Navy SEAL, you have been through more hell, and seen more bloody combat that I'll see even if I'm a Texas Ranger until I'm 80. So I'm not about to blow smoke up your ass. These animals are ruthless. They're smart, bold, and fearless, and they play for keeps."

Lt. Buxton stood up from his desk, shook Walela's hand and then Nick's, and said, "I pray you can find Tala and bring her home. Godspeed to you both."

The mood during their trip back home was gloomy. They needed to finalize their plans. But now, neither Nick nor Walela had much to say.

Finally, Nick spoke up, "You haven't said much since the meeting. I kinda felt that you were gonna volunteer to go undercover despite how I felt about it. I hoped that you would consider my wishes and change your mind, but I wasn't sure. For obviously personal reasons I'm glad that the Rangers cancelled that insane program. I hope that you realize just how dangerous your plan was."

"Yes, I do. I am sorry, I was being unrealistic. I had no idea how dangerous it was."

"Well, now that you know what's involved, what do you think?"

"I'm even more concerned about Tala's safety than I was before."

"Me too," Nick agreed, "But it would be suicide to blunder into that mess down there mostly blind. We need more intel. I wish we had someone on the inside, but we don't even know where the inside is."

"I have an idea," Walela offered.

"What?"

"I need to call my cousin, Noya."

"You've never mentioned her. How can she help?"

"Noya is a hacker."

"Really."

"Yes." Walela replied, sounding more hopeful. "Noya is actually a medical software developer in Atlanta now. But before she got that job, she worked as a freelance app developer and made money on the side as a hacker. It was not always technically legal, but nothing notorious either."

"So how good is she?"

"She is really good." Walela replied confidently, "And, she has never been caught…"

Concerned about discussing the plan during a phone call, texts or email, Nick and Walela decided to meet with Noya and discuss it face to face. But there was an additional danger with this plan, and it centered around Nick…

After he sustained his severe traumatic brain injury when the IED exploded beneath his SEAL team's vehicle in Afghanistan, he was transferred to Shephard Center in Atlanta for treatment and recovery. There, an experimental government neurosurgical unit called the Advanced Neural-Adaptive Research Facility, or ANRF, implanted an experimental computer chip in Nick's brain, providing his basic memories. The programming is accomplished by using a special laptop computer running unique software that communicates with the chip via a special wireless modem similar to Blue Tooth protocol. In time, the brain incorporates the chip into normal memory functions and the patient is unaware the chip is there.

Due to the physiological effects on a patient due to their mental attitude about their health, the team felt that it was necessary to implant the chip without the patient's knowledge. Nick knows his doctor, Dr. Benjamin "Ben" Aberman, a neurophysiologist, and his office staff, but has no knowledge of the surgery or any of the other members of the ANRF team. However, one of the team members is Noya Swiftwater, Walela's cousin and a software developer on the neural software development team.

Noya told Walela about one of their experimental patients, a "gorgeous hunk" named Nickolas Conner that her team had treated not long after she joined the team. After Tala disappeared, unable to find anyone capable of helping her find her sister, Walela conceived an idea. She found out more from Noya about the experimental surgery and programming process, and after much discussion and persuasion, Walela convinced Noya to help her reprogram Nick.

Walela discovered where Nick was working in Northern California, met and befriended him. She lured him to her motel room near where he was staying and drugged him. Then, Noya, using the ANRF team's special laptop, reprogramed his memory.

Walela had rented the log cabin near Balmorhea from a retired couple that were taking an extended vacation in Europe. She had taken Sprocket with her to California so that he could meet Nick and become familiar with him.

So far her plan was working, as long as Noya didn't slip up and say something about Shephard Center or the ANRF team during their meeting. There was only that one gigantic elephant in the room… Walela loved Nick, and he was only programmed to love her.

Walela had not anticipated this complication. She needed to know as much about Nick as possible, so she convinced Noya to provide her a copy of his medical file. She had not expected it to be so comprehensive. The file not only contained his medical history from birth to his most recent check-up, it also contained his personal history – information necessary to restore his memory. And Nick was a commissioned officer. A Naval Academy graduate and a Navy SEAL. He had a top secret security clearance. The military is very thorough in their investigation to determine acceptability for a top secret clearance. Walela learned everything about Nick, from his childhood to his time at Annapolis. She learned about his family and his friends. His deployment to Afghanistan and how he was injured. And his present job as a civil engineer for the US Department of the Interior.

Then she befriended him, which, according to Noya, was necessary in order to "prime his new programming", helping to enable a smooth transition when the implanted memory subroutine was triggered by the appearance of exit 192.

Walela spent time gaining his confidence, going to dinner, drinking and dancing, and going to movies, which would make certain she "imprinted herself into his deep memory". And somewhere during that process she fell deeply in love with him.

Walela suddenly found herself trapped within an inescapable quandary. At some point, hopefully after Tala had been found safe and returned home, she must tell Nick the truth. She knew, without any doubt, that learning the truth would break his heart and shatter any possibility of a relationship going forward. Just the thought of hurting him, of losing him, was almost more than she could bear. And what made it worse, she could almost see her grandmother shaking her head and saying, "Oh, my beautiful Walela. What have you done? What have you done…?"

Chapter 6 The Search Begins

Nick and Walela was busily preparing to travel to South Padre Island, Texas where they had originally planned to spend their vacation.

Walela paused and wiped sweat from her brow. "I am hot."

"You certainly are," Nick replied playfully.

She smiled. "I meant physically."

"Me too."

"*Weather* hot, you horny goat!" She scolded. "What I am trying to suggest is; we're packed and ready. Let's go take a dip at the park before we leave."

"Sounds good to me! Grab our bathin' suits and I'll get a couple of towels."

A short time later at Balmorhea State Park, wearing a black, form-fitting, one-piece bathing suit, Walela did a perfect swan dive from the high diving board, plunging deep into the cold, crystal-clear water of San Solomon Spring.

She surfaced directly in front of Nick, who had been watching her from the side of the pool, put her arms around his neck and sighed, "This water feels soooo good! I could stay in here all day."

"I could definitely spend all day watching you swim," Nick replied.

She smiled, kissed him and then pulled him with her as she dove beneath the surface of the cool, clear water.

Several days later they were settled in a rented beachfront condo in South Padre Island, which was a popular beach destination on the Texas east coast, thirty miles east of the US-Mexico border entry point at Brownsville, Texas.

They rented Noya a room in a nearby luxury hotel. She flew in from Atlanta to Corpus Christie, then rented a car and drove the three hours further south to South Padre Island.

Nick and Walela had been relaxing and playing on the beach before Noya arrived. They both knew it would be the only peaceful time they would have together for the foreseeable future.

Early one morning, Nick suddenly woke up gasping for air, and sat up in the bed. Walela was startled awake and very concerned about him.

"What is wrong, my husband?" she asked as she touched his face to check for a fever.

"I was havin' a nightmare. It seemed so real. I was at the wheel of my off-shore fishin' boat. I was runnin' fast out in the Gulf when I hit a submerged object and the boat capsized. I was underwater and couldn't get to the surface. I guess that's when I woke up. I remember backin' it out of the slip at my dock that morning. There's an old pelican that roosts on one of the pilings every night. I can still see my house on the bayou as plain as day. It all felt so real. That was my home. I know that house. I have most of a twelve pack of ice cold Dos Equis in the fridge…"

Nick wiped the sweat from his face with both hands and sighed. "I just don't get it. This is happenin' more often and they're not really dreams, they're more like flashbacks. It happens during the day, too."

Walela caressed his face, kissed him, and then pulled him down to her. "Rest now. Try to sleep. Tomorrow will be a busy day. I am here. Sleep and rest."

Nick's suffering was ripping her heart out. She continued to hold him as she silently cried herself to sleep.

The following day Noya arrived, checked in, and made certain the room had the internet connections that she needed. Then the three had dinner at a local seafood restaurant and went back to Noya's hotel room to begin planning the search for Tala.

"Before I get wrapped up in my favorite hobby," Noya began, "I want to thank you for setting me up in this gorgeous room."

Her room, with a living room, kitchenette, and separate bedroom was on the top floor and provided a panoramic view of the pristine white sand beaches and crystal blue water of the Gulf of Mexico. She opened the wide glass balcony doors to allow the sea breeze to fill the room.

Then Noya continued, "And I hope you appreciate what a pain in the ass it was to get a month's leave on such short notice. Fortunately, my boss loves me."

Walela hugged Noya and said, "I hope you realize how much we appreciate your help."

"Lea, don't misunderstand, I'm thrilled to be able to help," Noya offered, "But you know me - I complain about everything."

Walela laughed and looked at Nick. "When I stayed with them when we were kids, I would volunteer to wash the dishes. She would always complain because she had to dry."

"That's me," Noya confessed, then added "Nick, you haven't heard me call Walela, 'Lea' before. When we were little, I couldn't say 'Walela', so I called her 'Lea'."

Nick looked at Walela. "I like that nickname."

Then he spoke to Noya, "Since you haven't had a chance to see Tala's file yet, do you have any questions before we look through it with you?"

"No, but I have some comments. We know that the Cartels smuggle illegal immigrants across the border for money. We also know about the physical and sexual abuse that the men, women and children are subjected to by the Cartel soldiers and coyotes. The Border Patrol and ICE provides medical care for these victims. Surely the victims are interviewed to find out how and when they were abused and who abused them. If I could hack into those files, we might be able to gain information about these monsters. And that may enable us to get data on the operation of the Cartels."

"That's a great idea, Noya," Walela commented, then added, "Unfortunately, Tala's file doesn't have any information about abuse of illegal immigrants."

"Well, if we could get an idea who they pay the money to - who pays who - we could possibly follow the money." Noya offered.

"You have some really good ideas, Noya," Nick said.

"Thanks. Hacking is more about following clues and solving puzzles than anything else. I guess that's why I'm attracted to it. I love solving puzzles."

"But how can we track Tala's kidnappers?" Walela asked.

"That's more complicated," Noya replied. "The coyotes that bring illegals across the border are basically providing a travel service. Many officials of Central America and Mexico don't even consider what they're doing a crime. Heck, I've read that some of the Cartels bring the illegals to the border on large buses. If you don't count the physical and sexual abuse they receive, it only becomes a crime when they cross over the border into the US."

"But the thugs who kidnap anyone in the U.S. and then transport them across state lines violates 18 U.S. code 1201- kidnapping, a federal class B felony. Using or selling them as sex slaves only adds more felony violations to that. Those animals are much sneakier."

"Noya, you're not giving me much hope," Walela commented sadly.

"Well, my point is that the same Cartel animals that're smuggling illegals are also kidnapping young women and children. They're just two different operations of the same organization. You know damn well they're doing all they can to funnel as many of the unaccompanied children they're smuggling across the border straight into the sex slave industry. Those poor kids are ending up on the same auction block as the kidnapped girls from the US."

"Noya, you make an excellent point," Nick replied.

"Yes, you do," Walela agreed. "So, what do we need to do first?"

Noya opened her laptop and turned it on.

"Meet, Firefly. My baby. The Apple of my eye. Almost 32 trillion operations per second. A good friend – a bigger geek than me, believe it or not, built this for me. She has a ten terabyte digital hard drive, and as much RAM as he could possibly cram into her."

Then she pulled a black box from the bag and continued, "And just in case I had more need for speed, he built this modem for me. I can connect to cable TV, a phone line, or hack into any available wi-fi, and it will seek out a fiber channel, or the fastest path. It constantly hops from server to server to prevent me from being tracked. So, Lea, to answer your question, we fire my baby up and go hunting…"

In the following days, Noya searched across the dark web looking for any sign of human trafficking, young girls available for sex, and specifically, young girls fitting Tala's description. They were hoping that Tala would still be in Texas, or maybe Northeast Mexico. It was a long shot, but they also had to face the possibility that she could be anywhere in the world, sold to another sex slaver, or one of the many perverted monsters across the globe that buy young girls as sex slaves, concubines, or wives.

Noya was almost inexhaustible. This was her true passion. It was an irresistible challenge, but with a noble purpose. She loved her cousin, Tala, and worried about her safety constantly. She was determined to help return Tala to her family.

Nick and Walela could do little more than keep Noya supplied with gourmet coffee, energy drinks, and delicious food from a local deli.

After three practically non-stop days, Walela massaged Noya's shoulders and lamented, "I wish we could do more to help you."

Noya closed her eyes and bowed her head. "Aaaaah! That feels lovely, dear." Then replied, "Lea, you're doing great. Really. I've done marathon hacks before, but I've never had a pit crew."

"So how is it going?" Nick asked.

She pushed back from her computer, stretched, rubbed her tired eyes and replied, "Well, I've made a deep dive into the Dark Web. I've had enough offers of sex with children to keep a criminal court busy for decades. And I could've downloaded enough lewd pictures and videos to start my own porn site."

"Oh my!" Walela exclaimed.

"It's frustrating," Noya complained. "The Serpiente Cartel are apparently masters of keeping their sex trafficking in the background. They have a presence. But it's basically advertisements that they can provide safe and comfortable passage to the border. They run busses and charge several thousand dollars per person.

"Based on ICE interviews, the safe passage thing is a lie, unless you only consider arriving alive at the border. And that's not guaranteed. People are robbed. Females of all ages are raped, and anyone that tries to stop it or fight back are severely assaulted or killed.

"But, it's a paradox. They're known for their bravado. They make certain that their crimes are common knowledge, especially in the towns and villages of Mexico. Yet I've found nothing that ties sex trafficking to the Serpiente. It's as if that is the only crime that brings shame to the cartel. But, considering all of the crimes they're involved in, it's like a mass murderer being ashamed because he raped one of his victims. It just makes no sense."

"Maybe they're being cautious," Nick offered, "People are becoming aware of how widespread sex trafficking is. When children are involved, it becomes a very emotionally- charged subject. Many people could easily be triggered into vigilantism with the intention of killing the traffickers. Those Cartel animals would have to know that."

"You might have something there," Noya replied. "Drug traffickers and human traffickers are viewed differently than sex traffickers, especially involving children. That's a sick kind of evil. It tends to make a person want to put them out of our misery."

Noya turned back to her computer and said, "Well, I'm not done yet. There's *someone* out there in the ether, and their greed will be their undoing…"

******

Samson Block downed a shot of whiskey and stuck his fat Cuban cigar back into his mouth. Sitting at his computer, building a webpage filled with lurid pictures of young girls in various partially-nude or fully-nude poses, he scratched his crotch and puffed away.

Block blurred the faces and assigned false names and ages to the images to prevent identification. Most of the girls would eventually give their name and age to their captors, especially if they felt someone was honestly trying to help or comfort them. But in truth, it didn't matter. The customers wealthy enough to afford it were only interested in having sex with a virgin, or buying a girl outright. Otherwise, it was the lure of sex with a young girl, or fulfilling the sick fantasy of raping a child.

Block knew well which type of girls, and boys as well, brought the highest prices. He was an expert at producing a slick and flashy website. His skills and efforts generated a paycheck. The Serpiente needed his services. He wasn't going to get rich, but it paid the bills with some left over.

When his current project was finished, he would upload it to his boss, Alphonze Reale, for evaluation. Reale, a regional commander in charge of the Cartel's northeast border drug and human trafficking operations, would either suggest changes, approve it for posting on the Dark Web, or reject it. Rejection meant a do-over and Block rarely had to redo a web project.

He took the photos himself. And he liked to handle the merchandise. Reale was pleased with Block's photography, but not happy about his propensity to fondle, molest, and try to have sex with the girls. They were a premium commodity. Just like illicit drugs, high-paying customers expected a pristine, top-quality product. Block knew that. With possibly tens of millions of dollars at stake for just one girl, depending on how the auctions went, he could easily find himself with his throat slit for molesting the wrong girl.

So Samson Block had a side gig. He secretly collected the best photos, built himself a private website, unknown to his boss and the cartel, and sold the photos on the web. It was risky, but he needed the money he made from the photos to buy sex with young girls at a local brothel. That kept his proclivities in check and helped him resist the urge to molest the cartel's property, which helped keep him alive.

******

Reale sat at a table beside an elaborate swimming pool, complete with a waterfall and a Jacuzzi. Several bikini bottom-clad young women played and swam and he studied the screen of a laptop computer. Above him, the sea breeze rattled the fronds of the tall palm trees and filled the air with the fragrance of tropical flowers and a variety of fruit-laden trees.

The pool was connected to a giant, gleaming, multi-story Spanish-style luxury home sitting on a lush, sprawling, manicured landscaped estate along a high bluff overlooking the Gulf of Mexico. The name of the estate was Vista del Mar, meaning View of the Sea.

Pepe, Reale's houseboy and bond servant, brought a mixed drink and placed it beside the computer.

"Vamonos! This is not for you!" Reale barked as he continued to stare at the screen. "And get the girls more drinks."

"Si, Don Reale." Pepe replied obediently.

Pepe walked over to the pool and asked each girl what she would like to drink. Being a young man of 19, he very much liked to serve beautiful, topless girls. He was a handsome lad, something the girls made obvious by flirting and teasing with him. They were also cruel, as attractive girls can be. They had no intention of allowing Pepe any sexual favors. It was understood by each girl that she was there for Reale. Besides, none of the girls would consider wasting their time with Pepe. They were attracted by Real's money, and each one attracted Reale's attention during one of his many late night visits to a local club that he owned.

Reale attracted hot women like flies to a stable. Money tends to do that. Standing in line at the club, waiting to be admitted, the girls saw him drive up in his white Lamborghini Asterion, or the USSV Rhino GX, or another of his many high-performance luxury SUV's and high-end sports cars, or chauffeured in his Bentley Bentayga EWB Mulliner.

In his club, he had a special, glass-enclosed room in the loft. There he lounged on a large leather sofa, inviting attractive girls to come up, flirt and drink with him. When the club closed, he would have sex with them on the sofa, or take one or two of the girls back to his compound to have sex and sleep until noon. If he liked a particular girl, he would invite her to stay.

"There are no strings." He would always tell them. "Stay as long as you like. Swim, drink, eat, sleep. Leave when you wish. Just call Pepe, he will take care of your needs."

Reale also made it clear where in the house and on the estate they could and could not go. He avoided complications. But if a girl became too curious and wandered into the wrong place, security would spot her on the state-of-the-art surveillance system, direct her back into the area where she was allowed to be, and caution her not to wander again. A day or so later, she would be asked to leave. If a girl wandered into the wrong place and saw or heard something she shouldn't, she would simply disappear. The preferred methods were either a late-night cruise into the Gulf on Reale's yacht, where she would accidentally fall overboard, or she would be sold to a foreign buyer, never to be seen again.

Pepe hated Alphonze Reale. Pepe was smart and observant. He saw and heard almost everything, but reacted to nothing. It was impossible to judge his attitude by his outward behavior or expression. Pepe was stoic and patient. Reale, none the wiser, considered Pepe a stupid lackey.

Pepe knew Reale well, and didn't trust him as far as he could throw the Bentley. His father, José, was a drug mule for the cartel. Carrying large sums of cash made him become envious and greedy. He began occasionally taking small sums from payoffs when the transaction appeared to be sloppily done by a dealer that was drunk, or high on his own product. The occasions were rare. José was cautious and felt confident that he would not be caught. But Reale had a suspicious mind and arranged a sting to test his loyalty. José failed.

At first, Reale intended to execute him, but efficient drug mules were hard to come by. José worked hard and did his job well. Greed was expected in the drug business, so Reale told José that, since he had taken something of value from the cartel that was not his to take, the cartel would take something of value from him. Pepe's parents had three children, two girls, 14 and 11, and, Pepe, who was 9.

Reale decreed that the cartel would take their oldest daughter as repayment and punishment. The couple pleaded with Reale to change his mind and spare their daughter. Fortunately, the girl wasn't that attractive, so Reale allowed them to make a counter offer.

Without speaking to José about it, Pepe's mother offered to work as a prostitute in one of the cartel's brothels for a year to repay their debt. Pepe's father was livid and forbade his wife.

Reale pointed his finger at José and said, "Very well, I will do as I first intended and execute you. And your wife will still have to sell herself to feed your children."

José hung his head and cried.

Pepe suddenly spoke up and said, "Take me! I will be your bond servant. Take me and leave my family alone."

Everyone, including Reale, looked at Pepe in speechless surprise.

Then Reale spoke, "You are a brave young man. I will accept your offer, but only toward the punishment for your father daring to steal from the Serpiente."

Reale looked directly at José and said, "For repayment of what you stole, I will take the virginity of both of your daughters. Bring them to me tonight. They will not be abused, but they, as well as you, will always remember that the Serpiente is harsh, but fair. Our justice is always swift and severe. And your children will still have a father. My decision is final."

Chapter 7 A Glimmer of Hope

"Oh my God! I found Tala!" Noya screamed and jumped up, knocking her chair across the room.

"Where?" Walela asked as she ran to the computer with Nick right behind her.

"Look!" Noya pointed at the screen.

The picture showed a naked, golden-skinned girl, posed propped up with pillows on a bed, looking like she could be a centerfold in the gentleman's magazine of her choice. Her left leg bent with her toes pointed, just touching the bed. Tala could be Walela's twin, just considerably shapelier. Her face was blurred.

Nick, standing behind Walela, cleared his throat and stammered, "I really wasn't prepared to see your sister naked."

"Sorry," Noya said, then zoomed in to show her inner left thigh and continued, "Remember when we got our first tats. Tala was just 12 and we talked her into it. Lied to the guy about our ages."

Walela glanced back at Nick. "He didn't believe us for a minute. But he didn't care either. He just wanted to get up close to three hot Lolita's. I got a little uncomfortable when he closed the shop and locked the door. Then he said, 'I don't want to get arrested.'"

Then Noya pointed at a spot on the picture, on Tala's thigh just below what would be a bikini line and asked, "What does that look like to you?"

Walela began to cry, placed her hands over her mouth and said, "Oh God! It's her tattoo!"

"Yes!" Noya agreed. "That tiny red rose. From a distance, it looks like a mole. Fortunately, the photographer didn't notice it."

"I can see why," Nick observed.

"Hey!" Walela scolded Nick and elbowed him in the ribs.

"Well, who would notice a mole? She has a gorgeous body. Takes after her sister."

Then Walela looked at Noya and asked, "How did you…?"

"It's crazy. Sweetie, our prayers are being answered as we speak. God is with us on this," Noya began. "Having no luck finding anything of substance about the cartel, I decided to search sites that displayed pictures, thinking maybe I might find Tala or something that would indirectly lead me to her or the Serpiente.

"Well, apparently, the Dark Web search engines work a lot like the search engines we use every day. You know how you'll email, text or be talking about something on the phone and the next time you get on the internet there will be ads displaying links to the same something. Obviously, adware is watching or listening to and tracking users. I did a search and up popped an ad link to nude pictures of young girls. I backtracked the link and it's local. So, I was perusing the pictures and when I saw this one, she looked familiar.

"Just think, Lea. How many times have we seen Tala in a bathing suit?"

"A lot actually," Walela replied.

"Yes! We swam in the creek, literally, every day during the summer. We stayed in my pool every time you and Tala visited me in Atlanta. And I'll never forget that tat. We got in sooo much trouble."

Walela looked at Nick, "Our parents grounded all of us for a month."

"So, what now?" Nick asked.

Noya smiled. "I hacked into the primary server. There are hundreds of pictures stored on the hard drive. It looks like maybe three or four new pictures are uploaded to the site around the first of each month. And all the site does is sell the pictures. When you buy one, the blurred face is cleared up during the download."

"Let's do it!" Walela said.

"We'll need a gift card," Noya announced.

"Oh yeah, so we can't be tracked," Walela observed.

"Right."

"I'm on my way," Nick said as he walked out the door.

Twenty minutes later the download was in progress. They all stood anxiously waiting and watching the screen. The instant the download finished, Noya opened the file.

"Oh, thank God it *is* Talla!" Walela said as she breathed a sigh of relief, then commented, "Oh… she looks really pissed."

"Wouldn't you be?" Noya asked.

"I don't mean to rain on the parade here," Nick interjected, "but how do we know when this picture was taken?"

"It looks like the pictures are just added to the folder each month," Noya explained. "Tala's picture is the fifth from the last, so that suggests a time frame within the last two months – assuming the files are uploaded as soon as the pictures are taken."

"So how do we find that server?" Nick asked.

"Well, as I said, it's local. The ping is almost instantaneous. Whoever runs the server is a computer nerd, but they're sloppy. I'd bet the server is no more than 30 miles from us. And I'll also bet that it's in the same room as the computer this pervert uses. Give me a bit and I should be able to get map coordinates."

Noya worked feverishly, doing her hacking magic. Presently, she had a location pinned on the map. She brought up Google Earth and pointed out that, "It looks like it might be located in a warehouse-looking building just off the 101 in Matamoros. That's about 25 miles from here according to this."

"I need to get down there, surveil it and see what kind of activity there is. It would be great if you could get into the main computer," Nick suggested. "They might monitor building security on the same machine."

"I'll see what I can do," Noya replied.

Within a few minutes she had found the video security app on the computer and viewed the camera video.

"Oh man! That's great!" Nick exclaimed. "You are amazing, Noya!"

Then he pointed at the screen and said, "There's only one vehicle in the parking lot. Looks like an old, ratty Chevy van, maybe dark blue or black. So there's probably no employees or guards at the warehouse."

Then she paused and said, "I wonder…" and began typing.

"Wonder what?" Nick asked.

Noya chuckled. "Check this out. There he is. I just turned on his screen camera."

And there sat Samson Block, puffing on his cigar and staring at the computer screen. He had a fat face, a scraggly beard and wore a tattered tee shirt.

"He'll be easy to spot," Nick commented. "And he certainly won't be moving very fast. That guy must be as wide as he is tall."

Noya quickly turned off the camera to make certain Block didn't notice, then looked at Nick and asked, "What do you need me to do?"

"I'll go there and find a good location to watch the place. We need to be very cautious because there may be more there than meets the eye. I'll call you and we can coordinate when you turn off the security system and the cameras. We'll need to move fast to avoid alerting anyone. The problem will be big boy. He's our information source. Hopefully he'll be able to tell us how we can find Tala. After I've extracted from him whatever he knows, he has to disappear."

Both Walela and Noya fell silent.

"I know. It's something that neither of you had considered. I'll do my best to avoid unnecessary collateral damage. But you must understand that we're probably gonna have to break some eggs to make this omelet. And if things go sideways, we all could end up being arrested for kidnappin' and, or murder."

"That really puts things into perspective," Noya commented.

"I just don't want either of you to be blindsided by what's about to happen. This is not my first rodeo. This kind of op can go really well, or it can go sideways in all sorts of directions. That's why I want you both here, safe and secure, if possible. You'll be my eyes and ears. I may need to pull you in, but that will be my last option."

Nick grabbed his go-bag and turned to Walela. She looked into his eyes and quite literally fell apart. He was about to risk his life in an attempt to save her sister, a girl he didn't even know, in a family that he was not really a part of. The thought of what she had done was more than she could bear. As she fell sobbing into his arms, he scooped her up, took her to the sofa and gently laid her down, propped up on a large pillow. He sat down beside her, reached out and wiped the tears from her eyes, then leaned down and gently kissed her.

"I'm sorry," she offered. "I thought I would be stronger. If grandmother could see me now, she would be calling me 'udanila agehya'. That's Cherokee for 'weak woman'. It was something that she called us, when necessary, intending to make us girls stronger.

"Traditionally, Cherokee women were a powerful force in tribal life," she continued. "In many ways, women's status was higher than men. Grandmother taught us that, and tried to impress upon us how important it was to be forceful and stand our ground as women. I was impressed with the traditional Cherokee way of life. I thought it really made sense for women and men to share responsibilities and decision making. Cherokee men were still strong. They were warriors. But women not only ran the home, they owned it, and as elders, they shared in the politics and the making of laws of the tribe and the Cherokee Nation. In 1985, Wilma Mankiller became Principal Chief of the Cherokee Nation of Oklahoma.

"There was a Council of Grandmothers. My grandmother was a member. I'm so proud of who she was. And I'm ashamed of who I've become."

Nick gently turned her face toward his and said, "You have no reason to be ashamed."

She looked away and replied, "You don't understand."

"What do I not understand?"

"I'm keeping you from doing what you need to do. You need to go. Never mind me, I'm just worried about you."

"I'll be fine. Don't worry." He kissed her and said, "I love you."

Then Nick walked to his go-bag, picked it up and disappeared through the door.

******

Alfonze Reale finished reviewing the latest photo page addition to the website and texted Samson Block his approval and permission to proceed with the upload. Block received the text while he was in the process of making lunch for himself in the small kitchen attached to his office. Then he ate, made himself a large glass of bourbon on ice and went back to his computer to complete the upload.

The moment that he logged on, Noya saw it on her laptop. She turned on his camera briefly to verify that it was the same guy she had seen earlier. He was taking a long drink from his glass of bourbon. Then he picked up a cigar from the ashtray, relit it and turned his attention back to the keyboard. Noya quickly turned the camera off.

Nick processed through the border entry point uneventfully and continued south on Highway 101 through Matamoros, looking for the warehouse that Noya had designated on the map. It was early afternoon and traffic was light. He exited into the area of the coordinates and cruised around until he found a likely building, pulled over and called Noya…

"I'm lookin' at an old warehouse that has a parking lot similar to the one we saw on the security camera. I don't see the van, or any other vehicles. Maybe the van is around back. Do you have access to any other cameras?"

"Hang on…" Walela replied. *"And hello, I have Noya's phone."*

"Hello, Hummingbird."

"Yes! She is looking at different cameras now… there's the van. We can also see your car on one of the cameras, so you're in a bad location, especially if they're recording the video."

"Okay, I'll relocate."

Nick drove a short distance and pulled into an alley between two warehouses.

"Looks like I may be able to stay here for a while."

"Noya says that the guy is on his computer now. There's no audio, but she says the media player app is running, so he may be listening to music."

"I didn't want to do anything in broad daylight," Nick commented, "but we know he's there now. Ask Noya if she can shut down all of the security cameras for a few minutes."

"Yes, she can."

"Okay, just hang on. I'll drive back down there and let you know when to shut them down."

Several minutes later, Nick gave the command. "Okay, shut the cameras down and let me know when they're all off."

Within a few seconds Walela said, *"Okay, the cameras are off."*

"I'm going in," Nick replied. "Stand by."

"Be careful!" Walela urgently whispered.

"Why are you whispering?" Noya asked.

"What?"

Noya turned to look at Walela and whispered her reply, "Lea, you were whispering on the phone to Nick. He was in his car. No one could hear you except him."

Walela scowled at Noya, "Oh, shut up!"

Chapter 8 A Fat Source of Aggravation

Nick drove in and parked beside the van. Still connected with Walela, he had one more question, "Where is the guy now?"

"He's still working at his computer," she answered.

"Okay. I'll call you in a bit. Bye."

He quietly exited the car and walked to the back door. He could faintly hear music coming from inside. He quickly picked the lock and slipped inside. Nick's biggest worry was the fact that he was unable to bring weapons across the border. All he had was the Fox Folgore Rescue folding knife that he carried when he was on active duty with the Navy SEALS. Carried in the belt sheath, it was somewhat inconspicuous and very versatile. And it was the only weapon that he had - besides himself.

Once inside, Nick carefully closed the door and moved toward the sound of the music. He crept down a long, dark hallway and came to a door that opened into the cavernous warehouse with several large packing crates scattered about. The next door had a fogged glass panel. The light from within dimly lit the hallway and suggested the room was occupied. Nick eased the door open, carefully peaked inside and spotted the guy he was looking for, about 20 feet away, busily working at his computer. Nick pulled his knife, quietly opened the blade and bolted across the floor.

He caught his quarry by complete surprise, pulled Block's head back and put the knife to his throat. Block reached for a pistol lying on the table beside the computer.

Nick pressed the knife harder to his throat and simply said, "Don't."

Block opened his hand and slowly lifted it away from the gun.

Keeping the knife pressed against Bock's throat, Nick reached and picked up the gun, put his knife back in the sheath and checked to make certain the gun was loaded and ready to fire. Then he rolled Block backwards in his desk chair, spun him around, pointed the pistol at his head and asked, "You speak English?"

Block nodded yes.

"Who are you?"

"I'm the webmaster."

"I didn't ask *what* you are, I asked *who* you are."

"Samson Block."

"Well, Samson Block, you posted a picture for sale of a very special girl on your personal website. Are you also the photographer?"

"Yes," He replied, now sweating profusely.

"Then you know things about the girls, like who they are and where they are?"

"I don't know shit. I just take the pictures and upload them to the web."

"So these young, beautiful girls just magically appear on your bed, you take pictures, and the girls then just disappear?"

"That's about it."

"Look you fat pervert. Here's the deal. Either you're gonna tell me what I need to know, or I'm gonna take my sweet time beating you to death starting now, right where your sittin'."

"I can't tell you anything," Block replied in a pleadingly pitiful voice.

"Can't, or won't? The Serpiente won't have an opportunity to kill you after I beat you to death."

Block's eyes grew wide.

"Yes, I know you work for the cartel."

"Then you know they'll kill you, too," Block warned.

"Maybe. But you won't care because I'll have already beaten you to death. You're dying today, during the next hour or so, unless…" Then Nick slapped Block with the pistol and yelled, "YOU TELL ME WHAT I NEED TO KNOW!"

"Okay. Okay. I have a studio set up back there in my bedroom. They bring the girls here, one, sometimes two at a time. I take the pictures and then they take them away."

"To where?"

"Different locations. They have places scattered around the area."

Nick spun him around and pushed him back to the computer.

"Where's your cell phone?"

Block pointed to it, lying on the table near the computer.

"How often do you have to check in with your boss?"

"I've been working on an upload to the auction site. I'll need to let him know when the upload is finished."

"How much longer?"

"About an hour."

"Okay, here's what's gonna happen. You're gonna text your boss that your phone is about to die because of battery problems and you're gonna get another battery before the phone store closes. You'll finish the upload when you get back. Then you're gonna help me find the special girl I'm looking for. You got all that?"

"Yes."

Nick slid the phone to Block and said, "Get busy."

Nick watched as Block sent the text, then took his phone and said, "Now, bring up your website and page through the pictures backwards from the most recent. I'll tell you when to stop."

Block followed his directions. Nick watched and when Tala's picture appeared, he said, "Stop! Where is she?"

"I don't have a clue," Block replied.

"I'd be willing to bet that you don't like pain."

Block looked up at Nick.

"You expectin' to see a glint of mercy in my eyes?"

Block took a deep breath and sighed.

"You posted her picture about a month ago, right?"

"If you saw this picture on my site, then why did you wait so long to look for her?"

"Pay attention! Did you post her picture right after you took it?"

"Within a few days I guess."

"And you say you don't have a clue where she is?"

"What are you gonna do to me? Look, I just take pictures and run the website. I don't know anything. I've never even touched this girl you're looking for!"

"Lyin' to me will only cause you more pain."

Blocked sighed again and wiped the sweat from his face with his hands.

"Okay. If I help you, will you please not hurt me?"

"That depends on how helpful your help is."

"Jesus!" Block exclaimed.

"I'm fairly certain that yellin' at our Lord won't help your situation."

"Look." Block held his hands up in a pleading fashion. "Maybe I did touch her just a bit."

Nick scowled at him.

"Well, I needed to get her posed just right. She wouldn't cooperate. She's hot and I wanted the best shot I could get. My boss sometimes shows his appreciation when I do good work."

"Who is your boss?"

"Please! They'll kill me! These people are ruthless."

"Well, now you have two problems because so am I. Now, about that help?"

Block leaned back in his chair, wiped the sweat from his face once more with his hands, and then began, "The girl wouldn't give her name, so we named her 'Tika'. She's a fiery thing. Cussed me for everything under the sun. She's hot in all sorts of ways. That's probably why my boss took a personal interest in her. He brought her here for pictures, but he ordered me not to post her picture on the auction site. Then he took her back to his estate. I think he had me take her picture in case he gets tired of her. She can be auctioned quickly on one of the special events."

"Where is his estate?"

"It's on the coast, just off the Puerto Matamoros Highway. It's called Vista del Mar. You can't miss it."

"Take me there."

"Are you kidding me?!"

"Do I look like I'm kiddin'?"

Block slumped in his chair and sighed. "Crap."

"So," Nick began, "You're gonna drive me to my motel. We'll bring my wife back to get my car, then you'll drive me to Vista del Mar."

"You're an American, right? Your wife is across the border?" Block asked. "We'll have to go through the port of entry. They don't like me very much."

"You have a passport?"

"Don't need one. Dual citizenship."

"You wanted or something?"

"No."

"Then what's the problem."

"Like I said, they don't like me very much."

"Is your van clean?"

"I don't haul drugs, if that's what you mean. I'm an IT specialist."

"Then you'll just have to be extra nice to the border agents."

"Right," Block said as he rolled his eyes.

"Do you have extra ammo for this weapon?"

Block pointed at a desk drawer, slowly opened it and handed Nick two boxes of 9mm ammo.

"Well then," Nick tapped him on the back of his head with the gun and motioned toward the door. "After you, webmaster."

Before getting in the van, Nick locked the pistol and ammo in his rental car's trunk.

Getting across the border was relatively easy except that U.S. Customs agents searched Block's van from bumper to bumper while they questioned him for half an hour.

As they pulled away from the border, heading for the motel, Nick looked at Block and said, "They really don't like you."

"Humph," Block snorted and gave him a dirty look.

Nick called Walela and explained the situation. She was waiting when they arrived at the hotel. Nick got out and opened the side door for her. She sat down, looked around at the trash, beer cans and food wrappers, filthy windows, and an interior that had apparently not been cleaned in a very long time and said, "This thing is disgusting!"

"Sorry," Block offered as Nick climbed back into the van.

Walela looked at Block and said, "So you're the perverted bastard that took nude pictures of my sister and posted them for sale on the Dark Web."

"Yes," Block droned.

"If I could, I would kick you in the nuts."

"You're sisters for certain," Block commented sarcastically, "She did kick me in the nuts."

"Good for her!" Walela replied, then continued, "That name you picked for her sucks." "I'm not telling you her real name, but in Iroquois it means 'wolf.'"

"That fits," Block replied.

Nick looked at Block quizzically.

Block looked back at Nick. "Well, it does. She's as vicious as a wolf!"

Block drove them back to the warehouse. Before Walela returned to the motel with the car, she hugged Nick and said, "After you called and told us where the pervert thinks Tala is being held, Noya brought it up on Google Earth. That place is massive. It looks like it would take an army to rescue her."

"That's actually an advantage," Nick said, trying to reassure her. "They would never expect a lone infiltrator. Ask Noya to send me a link to the Google Earth page."

"Okay, I'll send her a text when I get to the border."

"Thanks," Nick said, then added, "There's a battle saying that goes something like, 'a running man at night with a knife can kill more sleeping soldiers than a hundred attacking warriors.' I'll find Tala."

Walela hugged him tightly, kissed him, and then said, "Just be careful, I have become rather fond of you." And drove away.

Block and Nick headed south on the 101 toward Vista del Mar.

"I have a satellite shot of the estate on my phone," Nick said to Block. "Tell me about the layout."

"I've only been there a few times. And I didn't stay long. But, I mean, think about it, with three floors and a basement, the place has a lot of rooms."

"How about security?"

"There's cameras everywhere. If someone goes where they shouldn't, a guard shows up and escorts them back to where they're supposed to be."

"How many guards stand a position or patrol the house and grounds?"

"I never saw any guards unless someone screwed up. I guess they rely on the cameras."

Presently they turned east of the Puerto Matamoros Highway. The sun was setting by the time they got near the coast. About a mile from the estate, Nick instructed Block to pull off the highway and onto a side road and stop. Then Nick had Block study the picture of the estate and point out various locations.

When they were finished, Block looked at Nick and asked, "What now?"

"We wait 'till dark." Then Nick reached into his go bag, retrieved a bottle of water, took a long drink and then handed a bottle to Block.

Block looked at the bottle in his hand and then stared at Nick for a moment.

Without looking at Block, Nick asked, "What?"

"I don't get you."

"What do you mean?"

"I know that you consider me the lowest animal on the food chain and would really enjoy beating the crap out of me. Or beating me to death as you have threatened more than once. Yet you give me a bottle of water and treat me decent, all things considered. What gives?"

Nick looked at Block and said, "I'm conflicted with all of this. I've been trained to view the enemy as a threat that needs to be taken out. It wasn't personal. They hated *me* and everything I believe in. But to me, they were simply the enemy. I did my job.

"But I've studied human trafficking. The victims are treated like animals. Kids are put into cages. Actually, animals going to slaughter are treated better than human trafficking victims. The animals aren't beaten or raped or deprived of water and food. They're not sold to others who will continue to abuse them or kill them and leave to rot in the desert.

"In my life I've never felt rage toward anyone like I feel toward you and your kind. I have no mercy. I can't think of even one reason why any of you should be alive. And I hate that you have made me feel this way. I've extracted many of my fellow warriors and civilians who were being held by the enemy. I simply did my job. I killed the threats that stood in our way and evacuated the friendlies to safety. Tonight, my goal is to rescue every person being held against their will in that estate. But in my heart, I want to kill every enemy soul I encounter. And that's not how I was trained. That's *not* who I am."

Block took a deep breath and sighed. "I didn't deserve that explanation, but I appreciate it, and I understand why you feel that way. I can't fault you for that."

After a long silence, Block said, "Thanks for the water."

"You're welcome."

Nick reached behind his seat and grabbed his go bag, checked the pistol to make sure it was loaded, and stuffed it into his waistband at the small of his back.

"Wish I had a few extra magazines," Nick said, thinking aloud.

"Hang on," Block replied and reached into the glove compartment.

Nick heard the sound of tape being torn loose as Block retrieved two loaded magazines that had been taped to the inside edge of the dash at the top of the glove box, then handed them to Nick.

Nick put the magazines in his go-bag and said, "You drove through the port of entry twice with these in your van knowing that Customs is suspicious of you?"

"I've done it before. I figured we'd be okay."

"U.S. Customs might've just seized the magazines and let us go. But if Mexican Customs had found even one bullet they'd have arrested all of us! You're an idiot."

"I've, uh, been told that before," Block admitted.

Nick sighed and shook his head, then opened the door and stepped out.

"So, we're done, right?" Block asked.

"Not even close. You wait here. Be ready to move. The friendlies may not be able to make it back to the van. If that's the case, I'll text you to come and get us. Don't even think about lettin' your boss know I'm coming, or leavin' me stranded here. If you do either of those, I will hunt you down and skin you before I kill you."

Then Nick darted away.

"Well, shit!" Block sighed and sunk down in his seat.

Chapter 9 Extraction

The fading sunlight still bathed the sky in orange and yellow hues, but deep shadows on the ground made perfect conditions for Nick to make quick and silent progress toward the estate. Scattered trees populated the area, but most of the plant growth was thick, jungle-like bushes and shrubs standing only a few feet taller than Nick. He ran most of the way, but then slowed to a cautious, stealthy, stalking pace when he spotted floodlights along the perimeter of Vista del Mar estate.

The lights were directed toward the grounds and the house, suggesting vanity landscaping, not security concerns. Nick carefully circled the perimeter of the estate, studying the house and the grounds, making note of the location of security cameras and sensors. Most of the cameras had overlapping fields of view. Then he found a lone camera on the back of the property, mounted high in a tree, facing toward the house. There were no cameras near enough to overlap the field of view, so he climbed the tree and swung the camera around, pointing towards a utility shed. Then he climbed the wrought iron perimeter fence, hurried to the nearest door, picked the lock, and slipped inside.

Inside the house in the security room, one of the two guards slept while the other monitored the camera video displays.

"Dammit!"

Startled, the sleeping guard woke up and asked, "What's your problem?"

"Well, it's actually your problem, that damn tree camera just slipped out of position again."

"How is that my problem?" The sleepy guard asked as he yawned and stretched.

"Because it's your turn to climb up the damn tree and readjust it."

"Idiots! I told the installers that tree was a stupid place to put a camera. I'll take care of it tomorrow after breakfast." He said, and settled in his chair to go back to sleep.

Just then an alarm light illuminated and a buzzer sounded. The monitoring guard silenced the alarm just as the sleepy guard sat up in his chair, rubbed his face with both hands and droned, "Where is it?"

"Exterior door near the back bedroom. Probably Pepe, but it might be one of the girls up to something."

"Okay, I'll check it out."

Once inside, Nick quickly locked the door and inspected it for security sensors. He spotted a sensor, but didn't see any cameras in the dimly lit hallway leading from the door into the house. Expecting a security guard to respond to the door alarm, he slipped into a linen closet and waited. Within a minute, a guard approached the door and checked to see if it was locked. Then he walked to another door just down the hall and peaked it.

A female voice suddenly yelled from within the room, "What do want, security prick? We're sleeping!"

"Did anyone just open the back door?"

"WE'RE SLEEPING! DUMBASS!" the female voice yelled louder.

The guard slammed the door and mumbled, "Bitch," then lifted his radio from its holster, pressed the transmit key, and said, "No problem here. Must've been a computer glitch."

Then he walked away.

Nick eased the closet door open, then crept down the hall to the door the guard had just closed, opened it slightly and slipped inside.

Suddenly the same female voice yelled, "Get out!"

Nick dove in the direction of her voice, quickly covered her mouth with his hand and whispered, "Shhhhhh! Quiet!"

She tried to bite his hand.

"Stop!" he whispered pleadingly. "I'm not gonna hurt you. I'm getting you out of here."

By then, other girls in the room were awake. Someone turned on a light and Nick whispered, "Turn it off!"

The light went out and Nick said, "Listen carefully. We don't have time to discuss this. I need to know where… dammit, what's that name they gave her? … Tika! Where's Tika?"

"Oh, you mean Tala?" One of the girls said.

"Yes!"

"She's in a room upstairs near the chief asshole's bedroom." Answered the girl who Nick had tried to silence. Then she continued, "I'm Sally. Who are you?"

"I'm Nick. I'm Tala's sister's husband."

"Damn! I was hoping you were single," Sally commented.

Nick looked at her in surprise and said, "Take me to Tala. But get dressed first. In fact, all of you get dressed. How many girls are in the house?"

"Ten. Us four," Sally replied, "Two with Tala, and three in the basement."

"One of you needs to go get the other three and bring them back here. Wear shoes if you have them and be ready to go, we need to move fast," Nick ordered.

Sally grabbed Nick by the arm and said, "Let's go."

She led him through the house and up the stairs toward the third floor. As they reached the second floor, a girl stuck her head out of a bedroom door and, speaking Spanish, asked, "What's going on?"

Nick turned to Sally, "Who is she?"

"Oh, I forgot about them. She's one of the three girls that the chief asshole picked up at his club. They're gold diggers."

Nick looked at the girl and replied in Spanish, "Get back in your room and stay there. Tell the other girls. You won't be hurt."

Nick and Sally continued up the stairs and entered a room across the hall from large double-doors that Nick assumed to be Reale's bedroom. Nick was certain that the guards had spotted them on security cameras as they moved through the house. When they entered the bedroom, the dim lights from the hallway provided enough light to see that only one girl was in the room. Sally went to the bed and woke her up.

"Where's Tala and Suzie?"

"In bed with the chief asshole," She replied.

Nick pointed at her, "Get dressed."

Then he turned to Sally, "Get back to the others as quickly and as quietly as you can. Watch for the guards, they're on the way. I'll get Tala and Suzie."

Nick peeked to check for the guards, saw none and slipped through the door toward the master bedroom.

Sally turned to the girl and said, "Just bring your clothes. We'll take the elevator."

"Who's *he*?" the girl asked.

"Married." She replied, sounding irritated.

Nick eased the door open and carefully crept across the floor toward the bed. The two girls were on either side of Reale. All three were asleep, and naked. He crept to the head of the bed and touched the nearest girl on her shoulder. She drew a startled breath as Nick placed his hand over her mouth and placed the index finger of his other hand over his mouth.

She nodded obediently.

Then Nick saw Reale slowly reaching beneath his pillow, trying to get to his hand gun. In a blinding movement, Nick pulled his weapon from the small of his back, pushed Reale's pillow against his head with the gun barrel and fired. A loud thump coincided with blood and brains spattering across the other side of his pillow, hitting the headboard and the adjacent wall.

Both girls screamed. Nick whispered, "Shhhhh!" but it was too late. He heard the guards running down the hallway.

Nick quickly grabbed Reale's gun from beneath the pillow and sprinted to the door. In seconds the first guard burst through the door. Nick grabbed his head and snapped his neck. As the second guard approached, Nick used the door as a pivot, swung both feet up and kicked him in the throat and the face. The guard slammed against the door facing, then fell to the floor, grasping at his throat and choking.

Nick had already pulled out his knife, but as he reached down, he hesitated. As the girls watched in silence, he looked at the guard for a moment, still coughing and gasping for breath. Then, with a quick flick of his wrist, Nick sealed his fate as blood spewed from the guard's slit throat.

Both girls screamed a second time. Nick just sighed and looked to see if other guards were on the way. Finding the hallway clear, he turned to the girls and asked, "Are you okay?"

The girls, still somewhat in shock, just nodded.

"Where are your clothes?"

"Uhhhhmmm, on the floor?" Tala answered with a question.

"Don't ask me, unlike you two, I'm not naked," Nick replied sarcastically.

They stared at him blankly.

Then he yelled, "Get dressed!"

Startled, they both jumped, and then scrambled to find their clothes scattered on the floor.

"We need to get the Hell out of here.," Nick commented, thinking aloud.

"That sounds great to me," Tala commented.

"Me too," her bedmate added.

"Do you have any valuables that you need to take with you?"

"We're not allowed to have any personal stuff," Tala replied.

"That figures."

Tala stepped into her shoes and said, "Okay, we're ready. By the way, who are you?"

"I'm Nick, your brother-in-law."

"What?"

"You heard me."

"I'm kidnapped by a bunch of perverts and my sister gets married?"

"Look, you can discuss this with her later. We need to go. Now!"

Then he looked at both girls to make certain he had their attention. "Follow me. If shootin' starts, hit the floor."

Out the door they flew, down the two flights of stairs and back to the room with the others.

Nick looked at Sally and asked, "Everyone here?"

"Yes." She replied.

"Where are all of the guards? I've only encountered two."

"And killed them," Tala interjected.

"He did. I saw it, too. And he killed the chief asshole!" Tala's bed mate added.

Most of the girls cheered.

"Everybody hush," Sally warned and then answered Nick's question. "There should be at least three more guards. But I don't know where they are."

"What about the staff? Cooks and such."

"They go home at night. Pepe takes care of everything then." Sally replied.

"Who's Pepe?"

"Oh yeah!" One of the girls said, "We can't forget him. He's a sweet kid. And cute, too."

"I asked, *who is Pepe?"*

"He's the chief asshole's slave. His bond servant," Sally answered.

"Where is he?"

"Probably in his quarters. He's been a slave for a long time," Sally answered again.

Nick sighed in frustration. "Where?"

Sally grabbed Nicks arm again and said, "His room is in the basement. I'll show you."

She led him across the first floor, through the living room, the den and the dining room, then down a hallway off the kitchen and down a flight of stairs, then finally stopped at a door. She knocked.

"Are you kidding me? Stay here!" Nick barked and kicked in the door.

Pepe jumped out of bed as Nick quickly crossed the room and pushed him back on the bed. "Are you Pepe?"

"Si."

By that time Sally had followed Nick into the room.

"Sally says you're a slave. Is that right?"

"Si."

"We'll, you ain't a slave no more. Your master is upstairs in his bed with his brains blown out."

Pepe pushed Nick out of his way, grabbed a pistol from beneath his mattress, and sprinted out of the room.

Nick looked at Sally. "Are we gonna have a problem with this kid?"

"No. He just needs to see it for himself. To know it's real."

Just as Nick and Sally got back to the foot of the stairs they heard three shots fired, then Pepe appeared, walking slowly down the stairs. He stopped about halfway down the last flight of stairs and looked at Nick and Sally.

"You killed him?" Pepe asked.

"Yes," Nick replied.

"I killed him again," Pepe declared, then raised his arms above his head and yelled, "Yeeesssss!" Then he leaped from the stairs, landing on the floor beside where they stood. Then he hugged Sally and began dancing with her around the room.

"I gather you're not disappointed that he's dead," Nick commented.

Pepe just smiled at Nick and then hugged him.

"Where are the other guards?" Nick asked Pepe.

"They went into town to celebrate. It was Carlo's birthday."

"When do you expect them back?"

"They must be back by 10 p.m. to take over the night shift."

"Damn!" Nick exclaimed. "It's 9:30. We need to go now! Do you have any valuables that you need to take with you?"

"Just a few."

"Go get them and meet us in the bedroom near the back door. Hurry!"

Pepe dashed away toward his room and Nick and Sally returned to the bedroom.

"Okay ladies, listen up. We have a van parked about a mile down the road. I've just sent a text to the driver and he's gonna meet us out front. Pepe will be here shortly. Then you're gonna follow me and do exactly as I say."

Nick's phone beeped. He read the text. *"Sorry Nick. Couldn't hang around. The keys are in the van. Good luck."*

"That son-of-a bitch!" Nick breathed in and let out a long sigh. "Change of plans. I no longer have a driver. It's just as well. He was your photographer."

"That fat bastard pervert!" Tala yelled. "I'd love to kick that asshole in the nuts again!"

Nick looked at Tala and said, "You're Walela's sister alright."

She gave him a quizzical look.

Nick addressed the girls again, "Gettin' to the van has just become a bit of a jog for y'all. I'll lead you through the woods and try to go at a reasonable pace. Just remember, we need to hurry. When the other three guards get back, things could get a bit complicated."

Pepe arrived in time to hear most of what Nick had said.

"Let's go," Nick ordered and led them to the back door and added, "Keep as quiet as possible."

He stepped outside, then motioned for them to follow.

Making their way through the thick underbrush was difficult. Most of the girls were clothed in flimsy attire, and wore sandals or similar shoes. Nick was as easy on them as he could be, despite the urgency of their situation. Pepe also helped the ladies, but now with an entirely different attitude. He didn't care if they were interested in him or not, he was a free man.

Finally they arrived at the van. Tattered, scratched, torn and exhausted. Nick had brought a case of water that he acquired at the border, and gave each girl a bottle as they packed into the van.

Nick climbed into the driver's seat, looked down at the steering wheel and found a note from Samson Block: *Nick, I'm truly sorry to leave you hanging. But I left my van. That's something, eh? I hope that you rescue the girls and that everyone survives. Tell them I'm sorry for the fondling. I'm a sick puppy. And please, don't hunt me down and kill me! Sam.*

Chapter 10 The Run for the Border

Nick cranked the van, looked into the rearview mirror and spoke to the girls. "Get as comfortable as you can. We're about an hour or so from the border. When we get there, it will take a while to get through Customs. They'll provide medical care for anyone that needs it. They'll probably insist that each of you get a thorough physical exam. And you really should comply with that.

"I.C.E. Field Officers will need to interview you. Answer every question as truthfully as you can. Don't worry, you'll be safe once we cross the border back into the good old USA."

Just as Nick pulled the van onto the highway, a black Chevy Suburban met them, going the opposite direction. It was obvious that they were seen pulling out from the side road. Nick saw the Suburban's brake lights illuminate and floored the accelerator, which made very little difference. The van was in poor mechanical condition, and the heavy load of twelve people didn't help.

Much to Nick's surprise, the Suburban's brake lights went out and it continued on toward Vista del Mar. Still, he continued pushing the van as fast as it would go. Fifteen minutes into the trip, he saw bright lights in the rearview mirror rapidly approaching.

"Crap." Nick mumbled quietly to himself. Then reached down, lifted up his go-bag and handed it to Tala, sitting in the passenger seat.

"What's this?" She asked.

"Do you know how to shoot?"

"Sure. My dad and brothers taught me."

"Good. I'm gonna be busy drivin'." Nick motioned toward the rear with his thumb. "We're about to have some unfriendly company."

Tala looked and saw the headlights in the distance.

Then she looked at Nick and said, "About the deal in the bedroom, we went along because we had to. He said he'd let the guards have us if we didn't do what he wanted. We were planning to get his gun."

"That was a good plan. A prisoner should always try to escape, but he would've most likely killed you both." Then he reached out, cradled her face in his hand and said, "It's okay. Everything's gonna be good, you'll see."

Then Nick reached into the go bag and handed her Block's pistol and the two loaded magazines.

"There's another sidearm and more ammo in the bag. Thankfully we only need nine mil. No need to conserve. They're gonna be throwin' a lot more lead at us than you will at them. Just keep your head down. And pray."

Then he yelled to the others. "It's time to get as flat on the floor as you can and stay there! Things are about to get real."

Just at that moment, the rear windows shattered as a spray of automatic gunfire raked across the rear of the van. Bullets ricocheted around the van and several rounds penetrated the front windshield.

Tala gripped the pistol with both hands, then leaned out of the passenger window in order to steady her arms on the side of the van and fired several shots. The right headlight of the Suburban shattered. She fired several more rounds, hitting the windshield. The guard in the passenger seat was holding his weapon outside of the passenger window. He suddenly dropped the rifle and his head fell forward.

"Good shot!" Nick yelled.

"I told you I could shoot!" Tala yelled back.

The Suburban came closer to the back of the van and Nick yelled, "He's trying to get close enough to do a PIT maneuver on us. Back 'em off!"

Tala turned around, kneeled in the seat and unloaded the pistol at the Suburban. The shots peppered the windshield and the driver slammed on brakes.

"Good job!" Nick yelled.

Tala looked at him and smiled, then shoved another magazine into the gun. A blast of automatic gunfire sprayed through the van again. Another guard had replaced the first one, leaning out of the passenger window and firing. Nick saw sparks in the right rearview mirror and yelled at Tala, "He's trying to hit our right rear tire! Take 'em out, take 'em out!"

Again Tala leaned out of the window and began firing. Just then the guard shooting at them ran out of ammo. Tala zeroed in on the guard and continued firing. He fell back in his seat and then slumped over dead.

"Sweetheart, you are amazing!" Nick announced, then cautioned her, "Watch the driver. He can't drive and shoot well. He's gonna try to ram us for sure."

Tala retrieved the other pistol out of the bag, handed the ammo and a magazine to one of the girls, then climbed over the other girls in order to get to the back windows and started firing at the driver. He swerved wide into the oncoming lane and accelerated, trying to get alongside the van. Tala kept firing at him until he moved forward and became blocked by the driver's side of the van, which had no windows.

"Crap!" Tala yelled and scrambled forward, hoping to be able to fire around Nick from the driver's window.

Just then another vehicle approached, meeting the Suburban head-on. The driver swerved onto the left shoulder of the road, barely missing the oncoming car as it flew past between the van and the Suburban.

"Whew!" Nick exclaimed. "Damn that was close."

"You're telling me!" Tala said from near his right ear from directly behind his seat.

The Suburban driver swerved back toward them and slammed into the side of the van. The impact knocked Tala to the floor and on top of two of the girls. Much to the driver's surprise, the van hardly moved. He failed to estimate the weight of the van, which was over loaded with passengers. It was several hundred pounds heavier than the Suburban.

Nick realized what just happened and saw a bridge approaching. The driver kept the Suburban along side the van, convinced that he could knock the van off the road and cause a roll-over. Just as the two vehicles crossed the threshold of the bridge, the Suburban driver made his move, thinking he could force the van through the railing.

Nick yelled, "Everybody hang on!" and slammed the van hard into the Suburban. The force of the impact, coupled with the additional weight of the van, shoved the Suburban into the bridge railing. This was a suspension bridge, with an overhead support structure. Just as the Suburban impacted the bridge railing, it plowed into one of the suspension pilings at over 70 miles per hour. The van kept going, but the piling bore the full impact of the left fender and part of the engine compartment of the Suburban, pushing the steering column through the driver and into the back seat. The impact ruptured the main fuel tank and the Suburban exploded into a ball of fire.

Everyone saw the flash of the explosion as it lit up the inside of the van and looked up just in time to see the Suburban experience a thunderous, fiery secondary explosion from the auxiliary fuel tank that provided addition fuel range.

Tala kissed Nick and hugged him as he announced, "Ladies and gentlemen that concludes our pyrotechnic display. We hope you have enjoyed the excitement thus far in our journey. Please relax now and enjoy a peaceful cruise for the remainder of our trip."

Everyone cheered and applauded.

The remainder of the trip had been going smoothly considering that the van no longer had windows and the windshield had a dozen bullet holes in it. But they were dealing with the wind and limited visibility well enough.

About ten minutes after Nick had transitioned onto the 101, he spotted another black Suburban following them. He kept changing lanes and each time he did, the Suburban changed lanes, staying behind them.

Nick reached over and placed his hand on Tala's shoulder. "Get the pistols and reload the magazines, Gunfighter. I think we have a problem."

She complied and turned around to kneel in her seat to get a better view of the new threat.

Suddenly, Nick spotted a guy stand up through the moon roof of the Suburban. Then he raised up a large weapon and brought it to his shoulder. Nick recognized it immediately because he had fired the weapon many times. It was a Mk-153 shoulder-launched multipurpose assault weapon.

Tala leaned out of the window again and opened fire, but it was too late.

Nick yelled, "Everyone get down! When I yell 'incoming', plug your ears and brace for an explosion!"

Nick watched to see if the weapon used a 9mm ballistic sighting round, or a laser sight. When he saw the laser illuminate he yelled, "Incoming!"

The weapon fired, Nick saw the missile launch and swerved to the left. It flew past them and hit the rear of a box truck just ahead in the same lane. The box truck exploded and pieces of it scattered across the roadway. Nick quickly swerved further to the left and got around the burning truck as other cars crashed into the wreckage and debris.

He looked back, hoping that the Suburban had been stopped by the mangle of crashing traffic, but he spotted it again, approaching fast. The border was approaching fast also. Only a few miles more and they would have the safety of US border behind them.

Tala leaned out of the window, aimed at the guy with the Mk-153 and opened fire again.

Nick saw the laser illuminate for the second time and again he yelled, "Incoming!"
Tala dove into the floor in front of the seat. This time Nick swerved to the right.

The missile hit the left rear corner of the van with a loud bang, but didn't explode. The impact deflected the projectile upward at a steep angle. Nick thought for a moment that it was a dud that failed to detonate. Suddenly it exploded directly above the van. The blast was deafening. The shockwave shattered the van's damaged windshield and almost knocked Nick unconscious. At the same moment the shrapnel from the exploding projectile sprayed the top of the van like a shower of hot metal hail. Some of the pieces pierced the roof and hit several of the girls. Tala was hit in the left shoulder.

Vehicles and passengers all around them were hit with the shrapnel or damaged by the impact of the shockwave. Behind them a semi-tractor blew a front tire and the driver lost control. The rig jackknifed and as the trailer swung around, it hit the Suburban from the rear like a bat hitting a baseball. The Suburban rolled multiple times down the highway, throwing the guy through the moon roof along with the weapon he had been holding. He was crushed as the Suburban continued to tumble before finally coming to rest on its top.

Emergency services, Federales (Mexican Federal Police) and Mexican Military personnel were arriving on the scene of the accident just as Nick limped the van into the US port of entry and asked for emergency medical assistance. US Customs and Border Patrol arranged for everyone to be treated in the same medical ward at Valley Regional Medical Center in Brownsville.

A short time later, Nick got a full briefing from the director of Valley Regional on the medical status of the girls and Pepe. The doctor reported that their injuries were limited to cuts and mild burns caused by shrapnel from the rocket blast. Tala's wound was not severe. Thankfully, the roof of the van absorbed most of the impact of the blast.

As for the condition of the girls as a result of their captivity, all of the girls showed varying indications of both physical and sexual abuse. Each girl received a thorough physical and psychological evaluation to determine their level of physical and emotional trauma. They would need time to heal physically, as well as emotionally. So, a determination was made for each girl's recovery based on whether she had a caring family or a safe refuge and the nearest facility where she could receive treatment tailored to fit her specific needs.

Nick and Tala were assigned adjoining beds when Walela and Noya arrived for their reunion. Noya set up a video call with Tala's parents and family. Walela refused to leave Tala and Nick. She slept in the room with them until Tala was released from the hospital.

The debriefing accomplished by CBP, ICE, DEA, US Marshals and the Texas Rangers gathered enough intelligence data from the kidnap victims, the data that Noya had hacked from the Serpiente website, and info provided by Pepe, to crush the Serpiente Cartel.

Names and identities of cartel members were released and several hundred were arrested with dozens more killed while resisting arrest. All of the girls and other kidnapped victims were rescued from the holding facilities around the area.

The discovery of the list of buyers also allowed international agencies and organizations to track down victims of human trafficking across the globe. In total, over a period of several months, more than a thousand victims of human trafficking were rescued.

When Samson Block finally got back to his computer and logged on, he discovered that not only was the cartel's website gone, but his personal website had been wiped out as well. All of his lewd pictures and pornography was lost forever. In the confusion created when Nick invaded his studio, Block made the mistake of leaving his backup USB drive plugged into his computer and Noya erased it as well.

One of the primary contributors of the intelligence data that enabled the Serpiente Cartel to be crushed, and the human trafficking victims rescued, was a nineteen-year-old boy named Pepe. He was smart and observant, stoic, and patient. And finally, after ten long years, Pepe got his revenge and was reunited with his family.

Chapter 11 Flashbacks

After only a few days, Tala was released from the hospital. Walela and Noya took her home to help her get settled back in to family life again, and they wanted to see that she was in a proper psychological counselling program to help her through the healing process.

Nick remained in the hospital recovering from the rocket blast. Walela intended to return as soon as she got Tala safely home and in recovery.

As Nick slept in the hospital, recovering from the injuries he sustained from the detonation of the rocket projectile that exploded directly above the van as he tried to reach the US border, he began waking up during the night, frightened and in a cold sweat. He was seeing images that he didn't understand.

At first, Nick thought that he was just having nightmares associated with the rescue. He felt that experience was enough to cause flashbacks to his combat experiences. His doctors at Valley Regional Medical Center agreed. They recommended medications that would relax his mind and allow him to recuperate normally.

But then he began to have flashbacks during the day. He would see images of the sea, sailboats and powerboats. Docks and boardwalks. A home on the water. Scenes of fishing and swimming. The visions weren't scary or troubling, but just didn't fit with the memories that he had.

Nick had not contacted his parents to let them know that he was in the hospital. In fact, they thought that he was still working on projects with the Bureau of Land Management. Upon his release from Shephard Center, Nick's neurophysiologist was concerned that after such a long rehabilitation, during which he was unable to manage any part of his life, the tendency to rely on his parents to make every important decision was very high.

The doctor felt that Nick needed to return to an independent life in order to rebuild his confidence and belief that he could lead a normal life again. And, as much as it pained his parents to take a 'hands-off' stance, they accepted the premise and left it up to Nick to contact them.

As a result, Nick had not been a very good son. Months had passed since he had contacted his parents. He had also missed two quarterly checkup appointments with Shephard Center.

Walela had set him up with a new smartphone and a new number, so callers only got voicemail when calling his old number. When his parents and Shepard Center contacted his boss, they were told that he had taken an extended leave of absence and requested no contact. Consequently, neither his family, the BLM, nor his doctor knew of his whereabouts. Fortunately, Walela moved his contact information into his new phone.

One day he was walking around the halls of the hospital and passed by the MRI lab. Suddenly he became very dizzy, which caused him to fall and hit his head on the tile floor. He was rushed to the ER and x-rays were taken of his head injury while he was still unconscious. He had received a concussion, but no brain-bleed injury was detected.

When Dr. Tim Wright, a neurologist, viewed Nick's x-ray, he was stunned. He immediately called his colleague, Dr. Ron Weeks, a neurosurgeon.

"Hey Ron, you busy?"

"Not swamped. What you got?"

"I'm in the Radiology Lab. You need to get down here. You won't believe this."

"Really?" Ron replied, sounding intrigued. "I'll be right there."

When Ron arrived, Tim was staring at the computer display. He pointed at a spot in the picture and said, "Check that out."

Ron leaned closer, then zoomed the picture in. "That's some kind of object. Shrapnel from a war wound?"

"Look closer."

"It's strangely symmetrical. Atypical of a piece of shrapnel. And there's no sign of scar tissue. So how did it get there?"

"Beats me," Tim replied, then pointed at the image again and asked, "But, doesn't that look like a wire or lead of some kind coming out of it? It does to me."

"I… don't know about that," Ron said doubtfully as he carefully studied the image. "One thing is certain. It's deep in his brain, just beneath the hippocampus. That will be tricky."

"He was just outside the MRI lab when he collapsed. Indications are that he had a seizure. The magnetic field could have caused that thing to move, especially if it's a piece of steel shrapnel," Tim suggested.

"Assuming an MRI was in progress," Ron added. "But the magnetic field is supposed to be isolated."

"You think we should try to remove it?" Tim asked pensively.

"That would be premature at this point, but the object might be the cause of his seizure," Ron suggested.

"I'll schedule a CT," Tim said.

"Good idea," Ron agreed.

Nick regained consciousness shortly after the x-ray. The following day, Dr. Wright was with Nick in a preparation area of the Radiology Lab, doing the preliminary preparations for the CT scan on Nick. He was lying on a gurney and Dr. Wright was standing beside him.

Just then an orderly walked by, suddenly stopped and looked around quizzically. Then he looked at Nick, moved slightly toward him, then backed away, pulled an ear pod out of his ear and stared at it.

Dr. Wright noticed his odd actions and asked, "Young man, is there something wrong?"

The orderly looked at Dr. Wright strangely and replied, "Man, this is freaky."

"What is freaky?"

"I was just listening to tunes. When I walked by, all I heard was this freaky noise. It gets louder the closer I get to your patient. And the sound is really freaky, like it's from outer space or something."

"Do you mind if I listen?" Dr. Wright asked.

"Not at all, doc, be my guest."

The orderly handed Dr. Wright an ear pod. When he placed it in his ear, he heard a trilling sound. And just as the orderly had said, the sound grew louder the closer he got to Nick.

Nick looked at Dr. Wright and asked, "What's goin' on, doc?"

Dr. Wright removed the ear pod and stared at it for a moment, then looked at the orderly. "You're right. This is freaky."

"What's freaky?" Nick asked, sounding more concerned.

Then Dr. Wright walked away from Nick and stepped into the hallway. Putting the ear pod back to his ear, very faint music could be heard. Then he motioned to the orderly, "Walk toward me," The music grew louder as the orderly approached.

"Okay, now let's both walk toward Mr. Conner."

As they got closer to Nick, the music faded into the trilling noise, which grew louder the closer he got to Nick.

Nick looked at Dr. Wright and asked, "What the Hell is goin' on?"

Dr. Wright simply placed the ear bud in Nick's ear.

"What the hell is that noise?!"

"It's coming from you," Dr. Wright said matter-of-factly. "The Bluetooth ear bud is receiving it from you."

"I'm some kind of damn transmitter?"

Dr. Wright didn't answer. He was on his phone calling Dr. Weeks. "Ron, I'm in the Radiology prep room. You need to get down here. STAT."

Several minutes later Dr. Weeks walked into the room. "What's the emergency, Tim?"

He placed the ear bud in Dr. Week's ear and proceeded to demonstrate the emergency.

Dr. Weeks handed the ear bud back to the orderly. "Thanks. Your term is 'freaky'?"

"Yes, sir."

"It's not just freaky, it's crazy," Dr. Weeks commented as he rolled an exam stool out and sat down. Then he looked at Nick and said, "We need to get the CT scan done now."

"Fine with me," Nick replied. "I wanna know what the hell is goin' on!"

An hour later, the doctors, the radiology technician, several other staff members, several nurses and the orderly that discovered the "freaky noise" all huddled around the computer screen in the Radiology Lab, viewing Nick's CT scan.

"This is amazing," Dr. Weeks said.

"It's a computer chip!" Dr. Wright exclaimed.

"Sure looks like one," The lab tech agreed.

"What is a computer chip doing inside his brain?" A nurse asked.

"Good question," Dr. Weeks replied.

"Why don't we ask Dr. Ben Aberman at Shepard Center in Atlanta?" Nick suggested from the back of the room.

Everyone turned to look at Nick.

"Who's he?" Dr. Wright asked.

"He's a neurophysiologist, one of the doctors that treated my severe traumatic brain injury."

"Don't you mean a neurologist?" Dr. Weeks asked.

"I had a neurologist. I also had a neurophysiologist," Nick replied.

"Why would you need a neurophysiologist for a severe traumatic brain injury?" Dr. Wright asked.

"Beats me," Nick replied. "Why don't you ask him?"

Everyone looked at Dr. Wright.

He looked at Nick. "What is his number?"

Nick recited it and moments later, Dr. Aberman answered.

"Hello, Dr. Aberman. I'm Dr. Tim Wright, a neurologist at Valley Regional Medical Center in Brownsville Texas. I'm calling about your patient, Nickolas Conner."

"Nick?" Dr. Aberman replied. *"He has missed two periodic checkups. Is he okay? We are very concerned. How is he doing?"*

"Nick is my patient. He received a head injury from a fall. We just ran a CT scan of his brain and we found… well, something unusual."

"He was supposed to inform you that no radiological tests should be performed on his cranium without consulting me first."

"Well, Dr. Aberman, in his defense, Nick was unconscious when we did the x-ray. Apparently, he forgot your order about radiological tests. The CT was done nevertheless, and I… or rather we, need some explanation. We've discovered what is apparently a computer chip located near the hippocampus, and I'm at a loss to explain it."

There was a long silence.

"Dr. Aberman, are you still there?"

"Yes. Yes." Dr. Aberman replied. *"I'll be on the next flight to Brownsville. I'll advise you of my schedule. Goodbye."*

"He's coming here right away," Dr. Wright informed everyone. Then he looked at Nick and said, "Mr. Conner, you are apparently a very important patient."

Two days later, Dr. Wright picked up Dr. Aberman at the airport. A meeting was arranged in Dr. Wright's office. Dr. Aberman greeted Nick warmly and sat down facing him to discuss his medical condition.

"It is gratifying to see you, Nick. I was concerned when you missed your last two checkups. And your parents are worried as well."

"I've been a tad busy, Doc. I'll call my folks. That's my bad. But, speakin' of checkups…"

"Ah, yes, your CT scan. Most unfortunate. But now that you're aware of the implant, I must encourage you to embrace it. Please do not be concerned about the functioning of this device. It has performed perfectly."

"Performed perfectly doin' what?"

"During your recovery from the severe traumatic brain injury, it became very apparent that your memory functions were not returning. The Advanced Neural-Adaptive Research Team at Sheppard Center reviewed your case and determined that you were a perfect candidate for the experimental Memory Enhancement Module. We gathered as much information about your past as humanly possible from your family, friends, fellow academy classmates and SEALS, encoded that information into the MEM, or 'module' as I call it. There are other memory-associated functions programmed into the module as well. Then we implanted the module in your brain and tied it into the areas that control memory.

"The results were almost immediate. We were all astounded. The programmed memory stimulated your long-term and short-term memory, your explicit or conscious memory, your implicit or unconscious memory, episodic memory and semantic or general knowledge memory. Thankfully, your motor skills were never an issue. You began recalling memories that we believed you had permanently lost. Your brain combined the module memory software with your normal brain function, just as we hoped would happen. For example, your math skills increased exponentially."

"Is that why I suddenly understand algebra and trig now?"

"Precisely."

"So much for givin' credit to my academy math professor."

"The recollection of how you received your brain injury returned in vivid detail as well. And that put you into shock. We were somewhat prepared for that, but it took several weeks to work through it."

"That was rough," Nick commented darkly.

"The general consensus was that you should not be told about the implant. I disagreed. Especially after your ordeal with the brain injury memory. I felt that you deserved to know why that happened. But it was decided that you needed to believe that your recovery was typical so that you would return to normal life, unaffected by the knowledge the module was implanted in your brain."

"Then why am I havin' dreams and flashbacks of a coastal place that I'm remembering like it's my home?"

"Dr. Wright has given me a complete rundown on your present situation." Dr. Aberman informed Nick. "Your file indicates that you are single, have never been married, and the information that you provided to me when I released you from Sheppard Center was that you were moving to Destin, Florida."

"Doc, my home is in Balmorhea, Texas, where I live with my wife, Walela and my dog, Sprocket."

Dr. Aberman looked at Dr. Wright. "Please have my large case brought up from your car."

A short time later, Nick lay on an exam table in an exam room. Dr. Aberman sat at the desk, tapping on the keyboard of a laptop computer, connected to a unique wireless modem. Dr. Weeks had joined them.

"You see, gentlemen," Dr. Aberman explained, "The module, or chip as you identified it, is accessed via the encoding wireless modem using special software on this laptop. Apparently, there has been a minor malfunction of the decoding circuits within the module, which allowed the Bluetooth function of the orderly's smartphone to activate the Bluetooth transmitter within the module. That is obviously not supposed to happen."

"Obviously," Nick quipped.

"Just please relax, Nick. Close your eyes, take a deep breath, hold it for a few seconds, then exhale and breathe normally. I'm about to access the module, but you will feel nothing. Just relax. Sleep if you wish."

"Thanks, I'll just… relax."

Dr. Aberman began to run diagnostic routines and calibration programs, hoping to resolve the Bluetooth decoding subroutines within the computer chip in Nick's brain that Dr. Aberman referred to as "the module".

Dr. Aberman pointed to the computer screen, "I'm running system diagnostics, which should locate the communication anomaly and correct it. Since a random Bluetooth signal – in this case, the orderly's smartphone – should not be able to trigger the module's Bluetooth transponder, I expect it to switch to a secondary transponder. That should correct the anomaly."

He continued, "And here, I'm running a memory parity subroutine. Nick's belief that he's married and lives in Texas is very concerning. The module's memory interface protocol was designed to simply augment his memory. To fill memory gaps when performing tasks like managing financial accounts, or mathematical functions relating to his civil engineering duties. There are also memory augmentations for individuals; family, friends, etcetera, and memories associated with events, both distant and recent."

"Amazing." Dr. Wright said, sounding impressed. "The module's memory augmentation covers such a wide scope."

"Yes," Dr. Aberman replied, "The advanced design of the module, using Nano technology and biological memory cells, allows us to explore many previously impossible capabilities. As your CT showed, the module is just beneath the hippocampus, and attached by nano-fibers to it, the neocortex and the amygdala, each associated with explicit memories."

"Biological memory. Wow!" Dr. Weeks said in amazement. "But that makes perfect sense. The cells are kept alive and vital by getting nutrients from his own body."

"Yes, that is correct," Dr. Wright commented.

"While you're on this fantastic voyage inside my brain," Nick announced, sounding irritated, "could you please find out what the hell is goin' on with my memory?"

"Relax Nick," Dr. Aberman replied reassuringly, "The memory parity test should be completed momentarily."

Within a few minutes the screen began displaying reports of the diagnostics results, including displaying alerts and reports of memory anomalies.

"Ah, here we go," Dr. Aberman announced. "The transponder calibration was successful, which means the communication anomaly has been resolved. And the memory parity results are coming up. Huh, there are multiple memory anomalies.

"This is troubling; the resident memory file in the module is almost twice as large as the backup file on the computer hard drive. The resident memory has apparently been partially overwritten. According to the file properties, the file was updated.

"Nick, have you visited my office since your last checkup and I'm not aware of it?"

"No, doc. I missed my last two appointments and the one before that was over six months ago."

"So how is this possible?" Dr. Aberman asked. "Who have you seen from our staff?"

"No one, doc. I haven't been to Atlanta."

"Unbelievable," Dr. Aberman commented as though he was thinking aloud.

"So, has someone reprogrammed Nick's memory without his knowledge?" Dr. Wright asked.

Dr. Aberman looked at him in surprise and replied, "Yes, that is the only possible answer."

"Well, how the hell could anyone have done that?" Nick asked.

"You must have been either asleep or unconscious," Dr. Wright replied.

"Unconscious?!" Nick exclaimed. "Who the hell would want to knock me out?"

Dr. Aberman continued to search through the computer files.

"The log file should show every time the module has been accessed, and who logged on, but someone has attempted to erase some of the logs... there's a hidden file located within the logon security app that captures all logon activity. If I can find that file..."

Minutes ticked by as Dr. Aberman searched through the files deep within the security app.

Finally, Dr. Aberman announced, "Noya Swiftwater."

"Noya?" Nick exclaimed.

"Yes. She was the last one to log on before I logged on today. Noya has deliberately modified your memory, which is very likely why you believe you're married and living in Texas. I just found a backup of the files she used, hidden on the hard drive."

"Son of a bitch!" Nick whispered.

"It would be too dangerous to tamper with the resident memory on the module. Although the memories of your real life and home has been suppressed, I suspect that your realization of the truth will force those suppressed memories to the surface without causing any conflicts with the module memory files."

Nick's mind was racing. His thoughts were a jumble of the events of recent months, of Walela and intimate moments with her, of Noya and his project in Northern California. Suddenly he wasn't sure what was real or even for certain who he was.

He sat up and glanced over at Dr. Aberman. "I'm sorry doc, I didn't catch that last part."

Dr. Aberman stood up, walked over and placed his hand on Nick's shoulder. "Not to worry. You're doing fine. You have a lot to sort out. Take your time. There's no rush. You'll get through this with no problems. Just call me if you need anything."

Nick reached up, scratched his head and said, "Well, that explains my little voice."

"Pardon me?" Dr. Aberman said, looking at Nick quizzically.

"You know that little voice in the back of your mind that warns you when you're about to do somethin' really stupid?" Nick asked.

"Yes, as a matter of fact, I do," Dr. Aberman replied.

"Well, that voice has been screamin' at me quite a bit lately. I thought I was maybe havin' issues with my brain injury, but all of this explains it. That little voice was right. I should've listened."

Dr. Aberman looked at Nick thoughtfully, but said nothing.

Nick looked up at him, smiled and said, "Thanks doc. You know how much I appreciate everything you've done."

"Nick, why don't you return to your room?" Dr. Wright suggested. "I'll be down in a bit to check on you."

"Okay, doc." Nick replied and left the exam room.

Dr. Wright turned to Dr. Aberman and asked, "He needed your encouragement just then, but do you really think he'll be okay?"

Dr. Aberman sat down and sighed. "As I told Nick, I was opposed to keeping knowledge of the module from Nick from the start. I felt that he should know. But I was voted down. At least now we're past that issue.

"He's an amazing young man. A true hero. I watched him fight and claw his way back from the severe traumatic brain injury, yet he never uttered a hint of complaint or self-pity. For almost a year he didn't even know who he was. He spent time with the severely injured vets, helping with their recovery. He also spent a lot of time in the children's ward, entertaining them.

"He was a Navy SEAL you know? His entire team was killed in that explosion. I've talked extensively with his fellow SEALS, his commanders and his family. He's brilliant. A well-trained and truly fierce warrior, more capable of killing with his bare hands than I am with my deer rifle. Yet the compassion and gentleness that he displayed toward his fellow vets, amputees, burn victims and those even more severely wounded, and the way he related to the children was simply amazing. I would make my rounds, he wouldn't be in his bed, and I would find him on the floor in the kids ward playing with them and their toys.

"I don't know what's going on. This obviously has something to do with the rescue of those young women. One was his wife's sister, correct? He's certainly capable of accomplishing something like that. I just can't imagine how Noya could be led to reprogram the module. How could she do that to Nick?

"Tim, I would really appreciate some closure on this if possible. I think Nick has had enough thrown at him today. I assume I'll be seeing him on his next scheduled checkup, but I'd really rather not wait that long."

"I understand, Dr. Aberman," Dr. Wright replied.

"Call me Ben, please. You've become initiated into a very unique group. Your patient is a very special case. As I explained during our ride from the airport, my team with the Advanced Neural-Adaptive Research Facility does amazing research there at Shephard Center. If you're ever in Atlanta, give me a call."

"Ben, I look forward to it."

Chapter 12 Hard News

Nick sat on the edge of his bed. His feet were just close enough to the floor to tap his toes on the cold luxury vinyl tile. He stared at the floor, and thought. He thought about his dog, Fred, when he was a kid. A rambunctious black Labrador Retriever, his constant companion and accomplice in all adventures, mirth, and mayhem. Fred lived to the ripe old age of 15. He died in Nick's arms, humanely put down by the local veterinarian due to Fred's rapidly failing health. Nick never had a dog after Fred. Until Sprocket. And now, Nick wondered if Sprocket was his dog or Walela's.

He thought about his love for her. And the passion of their lovemaking. He had never known feelings for anyone like he felt for Walela. Now he wondered if his love for her was real or programmed by Noya.

Nick had girlfriends during high school. Some on those relationships became very heated. But then came graduation and his appointment to Annapolis. His years at the Naval Academy left little time for dating and romantic relationships. During breaks from classes he spent time earning his master scuba diver's certificate, a private pilot's certificate, a rotary wing certificate, doing cross-country endurance runs, and mountain climbing.

After graduating as a commissioned officer from Annapolis with a general engineering degree, it was on to SEAL training for another year. One of the proudest moments in Nick's life was being awarded the designation of 113X Special Warfare Officer and earning the SEAL Trident Pin, referred to as "The Budweiser" by most SEALs. Then there were deployments with his team, more training, special combat exercises, various missions, and finally, deployment to Afghanistan.

Now here he sat. His head spinning from the many revelations that had occurred during the last few hours. A computer chip in his brain providing part of his memory. And part of that memory is false. Intentionally placed there to fool him into believing that he's someone that he's actually not. And the woman that he thought he loved most was at the heart of it.

******

The following morning, Walela arrived at Valley Regional Medical Center unannounced. She had been texting and calling Nick constantly since she and Noya left to take Tala back home, keeping him up to date with her and keeping herself informed about his condition. But she didn't mention that she was en route to Brownsville.

She hurried down the hallway to the nurse's station, paused and asked, "Is Nick in his room?"

The nurse stared at Walela for a few seconds. The nurse had heard gossip about Nick's situation, which caused her to hesitate with a bit of uncertainty. A nurse standing beside her realized what was happening and answered for her, "Yes ma'am, he is in his room."

Walela sensed that something wasn't right, but continued to Nick's room, excited to surprise him with her unannounced arrival.

She opened the door slightly and peeked in, then stepped inside and said, "Hello, my husband! I missed you!"

Nick looked up at her and she ran to him and kissed him. His response was somewhat cold. She pulled back and asked, "What's wrong? Are you okay"

"Dr. Aberman was here."

"Who is he?"

"My neurophysiologist from Sheppard Center."

"Why is he here?"

"I've been havin' flashbacks. I had a seizure."

"A seizure?" Walela asked, looking concerned.

"Yes. I fell and hit my head. My doctor's found something in my brain. Dr. Aberman came to check on me and explain what it is."

"So you know about the chip?"

"Yes. But how do *you* know?"

"I've wanted to tell you and explain everything. I just didn't know how to begin."

"So, Noya told you?"

"Yes."

"I know about the memory modification. We're not really married, are we?"

Walela felt the strength go out of her legs. She grabbed Nick's arm to hold her up and sunk down on the bed.

"I'm so sorry, my love," she whispered, hugging his arm with her face buried into his shoulder.

"My love?"

"Yes!" She looked up at him and repeated pleadingly, "Yes! I love you. I fell in love with you almost from the beginning."

"Then why weren't you honest with me?"

"I was desperate to find Tala. No one would help me."

"You could've just asked me to help you."

"How could I ask a perfect stranger to risk his life to rescue my sister?"

"I rescued people in Afghanistan that hated me. I would've been honored if you had asked me for help. I'm honored that I was able to rescue Tala."

"You are the most loving, the most amazing man that I have ever known. I'm so sorry for what I have done to you. I said that I have not told you the truth because I did not know how to begin, but to be totally honest, I was afraid that when you learned the truth, I would lose you. Nick, I don't want our relationship to end."

"Our relationship never began. It was all a lie. I love you because Noya programmed me to love you. We don't have a life together. We don't have a home. My home is in Destin, Florida. You've never even been there."

Walela began to cry and tearfully pleaded, "Please, can we not start over? We actually know a lot about each other. Could we not pick up the pieces and begin making a life together?"

Nick continued to stare at the floor. He hadn't moved from the edge of the bed.

"I had a life. You hijacked it. I'm not sure I even know who I am now. You need to go."

Walela slid off the bed, wiped the tears from her eyes and turned to face Nick. "I will always love you. I do not know how I can make up for what I have done to you. I do not have the words to say what I feel. I just know that we are meant to be together and I will always love you."

Then she gently touched his face. "Whatever you do, wherever you go, take care of yourself and be well. May God watch over you always…"

Then she turned and walked away.

Five minutes later, Dr. Wright leaned through the door to Nick's room and asked, "Need some company?"

Nick was still sitting on the edge of the bed, looking at the floor. He looked up and replied, "Sure doc, come on in. Have a seat. I would offer you a drink, but they won't let me have alcohol."

"I have a confession," Dr. Wright said.

"Well, today is apparently the day for 'em."

"I, uh, heard part of your conversation. Toward the end there. I apologize for eavesdropping."

"That's okay. She was doin' her best to hang on to me. I just don't see how she can expect me to go back to a make-believe life and pretend that none of that crap that she and Noya did really happened."

"Nick, I can certainly understand how you feel. I'm sure I would react the same way. But you need to consider her point of view in all of this. She was afraid that she was going to lose her little sister in a most horrible way. She felt completely helpless. Plus seeing her mother and father worrying and suffering, as well as the rest of her family. You need to remember that a woman often thinks with her heart. Emotion rules a lot of their decision-making. She may be a very logical thinker when it comes down to it, but there was very little logic involved in her decision to, as you put it, 'hijack' your life to help her. And, based on what Dr. Aberman told me about the function of your implant, the way they made all of that happen is simply brilliant."

"So, you weren't aware of anything that happened to hijack your life?"

"Not really. A few things were happening that didn't make sense. I had some memories that really bothered me. That was probably the beginning of what became the flashbacks. But I truly believed that we were married and very much in love."

"And how much time have you actually spent together?"

"Almost five months I guess. I've also had some memory flashes of doing things with her while I was working on a construction project in Northern California. It's kinda foggy. It had to be before I got back home to the cabin in Balmorhea. I remember seeing Exit 192. I knew I was almost home. But… that's not home. Destin is home."

"It will take some time for you to get your memory straight. But you will. Dr. Aberman is confident of that fact."

"It's all just a crazy fog right now."

"Which is completely expected. So don't let it worry you. Just go with. Allow your memories to play themselves out. The false memories will be overshadowed by your real memories and will finally fade away."

"You think?"

"Oh sure. I don't just think. I know. I have this sheepskin thing on the wall in my office. At one point I had some doubt that I would actually get it, but here I am. I've come to discover that I'm pretty damn good at what I do. And I'm very confident that you'll be just fine. In fact, I had planned to release you on the day you fell and hit your head. Dr. Aberman, Dr. Weeks, and I have thoroughly reviewed your case and I submitted the paperwork for your release about an hour ago. It's being processed as we speak, so one of our staff should be here very soon to kick you out of this place."

"That's great doc. I really appreciate all that you've done for me."

Dr. Wright stood up and shook Nick's hand. "Nick, it has been a pleasure. I am honored to have met you and honored to have had the privilege to provide your medical care. I just want to say one more thing…"

Dr. Wright sat down on the bed beside Nick, in the same spot that Walela had sat. He placed his hand on Nick's shoulder and said, "You just told me that you and Walela have spent almost five months together as a loving couple. Can you agree with that statement?"

"Yes, I can. Those months were really amazing. I can't deny that."

"Well, I submit that, despite the covert and untruthful tactics that she used to bring you to take Exit 192 instead of continuing on to your home in Florida, those months that you spent together, and the love that grew between you during that time, is real. What I heard in her voice when she confessed her love for you was real emotion. That woman is deeply and hopelessly in love with you. You may not feel love for her right now. You're angry. That's okay. Just take your time. Allow your memory to sort itself out and then, search your feelings. What you feel deep down. I think you will find that she means more to you than you realize."

Then Dr. Wright stood up, turned and pointed at Nick and added, "And you have my number…"

Then he left the room. Nick continued sitting there on the bed. Staring at the floor.

About an hour later, a nurse came in the room and asked, "How are you feeling?"

"I'm okay, all things considered."

As she took his blood pressure, pulse rate, and temperature, she continued to talk, "As you know, Dr. Wright has released you. We're just about done. One of our administrative staff will be along in a few minutes with some paperwork for you to sign and then I'll be back to give you a free ride all the way to the lobby."

The nurse finished and was about to walk out the door, then she stopped and said, "Oh! I almost forgot. Your wife stopped by the nurse's station on the way out and left the keys to your Hellcat. She said that she had forgotten to give them to you. She said to tell you that it's parked right out front, near the main entrance. You can't miss it."

Then she handed Nick a set of keys.

"Thanks," Nick said.

He looked at the keychain and recognized it as his. Except that it had three key fobs, with an extra one that he didn't remember. He looked closer and realized that Walela had taken the time to remove the key fob for his Hellcat from her keychain and added it to his keys, but she left the key fob for her Raptor on his keychain, along with the cabin key and barn key.

Without uttering a word, she had made a very loud statement – 'I'm letting you go, but I'm still yours'…

Nick kept looking at the keys, then he put his hands over his face and wept.

Chapter 13 Home

The nurse came with a wheelchair and announced, "Your chariot to freedom, Sir."
She rolled Nick out of his room, down the elevator, through the lobby, out the main entrance door, then stopped and set the wheel lock.

"Nick, thank you for allowing us to provide your medical care. You've become quite a celebrity during your stay. We also had the honor of treating most of the young women that you rescued as well as the ones who were rescued because of your heroic efforts. Those ladies would elect you king of the world if they had their way."

Nick chuckled as he stood up and gathered up the paperwork. "I don't know about that. I just did my best."

"Well, your best is good enough for me. You are officially my hero."

"I am honored," He humbly replied.

"You are now officially a former patient of Valley Regional Medical Center," She announced.

"Thanks for the great care," Nick replied.

"Be well, my hero," She said with a smile as she turned and reentered the lobby.

Just inside the lobby, two nurses stood watching as Nick walked away. The nurse with the wheelchair stopped and turned to watch him as well.

"Is 'dreamboat' still a thing that we say about guys?" She asked the other two.

"I don't know," replied one of the nurses, "but that's the perfect word… dreamboat, and he could sail away with me anytime."

Nick unlocked the Hellcat and tossed the paperwork on the passenger seat. He glanced in the back and saw his luggage. He climbed into the driver's seat and spotted his Yeti travel mug in one of the cupholders. He looked closer, opened the lid and discovered it was filled with chunklet ice and sweet tea.

"Hummingbird, this is gettin' to be more than I can take," He said aloud.

He took a long drink of the ice-cold tea, and then finished his comment, "But I sure do appreciate it. You're a sweetheart."

He shut the door and sat for a moment in the silence, thinking.

She parked here. Where did she go? Did she take a taxi to the airport? Or rent a car, intending to drive home? She brought the Hellcat, planning for us to drive back home together. She probably wouldn't want to do that long, lonely drive back home alone. Even though she drove all the way from Balmorhea to Brownsville alone, she shouldn't have to travel back home alone.

Nick cranked the Hellcat and headed for Brownsville - South Padre Island International Airport. On the way there he wondered why he was thinking of trying to catch her before she left. He had just told her she had to go. Essentially throwing her out of his life. He was still so mad at her that he was unable to think of anything to say. Not that she would care. Maybe he just needed to tell her goodbye. To actually say it.

Arriving at the airport, he parked in the unloading zone at the first departure gate, ignored the sign warning not to leave your vehicle unattended, walked inside, and scanned the people, trying to spot Walela. Then he looked at the departure schedule. One of the listed flights was to Tulsa. The status indicated that the flight had departed ten minutes earlier.

People were walking by, many of them noticing Nick and taking second glances. Just then a voice from behind him said, "She's gone home to Muskogee."

Nick turned to find an older Hispanic man with kind eyes and weathered lines on his face, standing there, looking up at him.

"Did you just say Muskogee?"

The old man nodded. "You're wondering how I know that."

"As a matter of fact…"

"I'm Carlos, a part-time concierge. Fancy name for a baggage boy. I helped your wife with her luggage. Then she was having trouble with the kiosk. Automation."

He looked down and shook his head. "Everyone is in a hurry. I miss the old days. Life was slower. It was more personal. People cared back then. Anyway, she seemed a bit rattled and was getting frustrated with that computerized contraption, so I helped her buy her ticket to Tulsa. She had over an hour to wait, so after we got her checked in, we went to the coffee shop and talked for a while. Seemed like she needed someone to talk to."

"Thanks so much for helping her. I was worried about her traveling alone. But she's really not my wife," Nick confessed.

"Walela said that she hoped you might show up. She kept watching for you. She is quite a lady. Beautiful, smart, and full of fire. She reminds me a lot of my Maria. She sure was a fiery thing. But she's gone now."

"I'm sorry."

"Thanks, but there's no need for sorrow. We had a great life together. Met as teenagers. Had a bunch of kids. Got grandkids and great grandkids now. Too many for the house. We have to rent a hall when we get together these days. Maria and I had 67 wonderful years together. She was shot and killed in a gang-related drive-by shooting a few years ago. She died in my arms. The investigator said that Maria had probably been targeted because she apparently saw something she wasn't supposed to see. By an interesting coincidence, she was murdered by the cartel that you just helped take down. Maria would be very grateful and proud of you. So am I."

"Carlos, that really means a lot," Nick replied humbly.

"Well, I have to get back to work. Several departures coming up."

Carlos reached out both his hands and shook Nick's hand, gave him a warm smile and said, "About your thinking she's not your wife. Maybe you need to reconsider. A marriage is so much more than a piece of paper. Via con Dios, Nick."

Then he turned and walked away.

"God bless you too, Carlos!" Nick called after him.

Carlos just raised his hand, waved, and kept walking.

Nick stood there for a few moments longer, thinking about what Carlos had said and watching as he finally faded into the busy airport activity. Then he went back to his Hellcat, started the engine and headed for Destin.

It was a long drive from Brownsville. His Dodge Durango SRT Hellcat was somewhat of a sleeper and looked like any other mid-sized SUV. Only the small SRT badge suggested it was a bit more than a typical Durango. He had become accustomed to drivers who recognized it, thought they had hot cars, and attempted to challenge him to an impromptu race.

Nick liked to drive fast and race. He knew his Hellcat was faster than most cars on the road, but he was not in the mood. Although he had multiple challengers, he simply ignored them and plodded along near or just above the posted speed limit. At least that helped somewhat with the gas mileage, but Nick really didn't care about that either. Nick was deep in thought. Still trying to sort out the jumbled mess that resulted from the discovery of the "module" in his brain and the deviousness of Walela.

He called his parents, apologized for not keeping in touch and explained everything. They were delighted to hear his voice and very supportive. Just talking to them helped brighten his mood, and it triggered more memories as well.

He tried to get some rest at each food and fuel stop. He would find a dark parking space, recline in his seat and close his eyes, but his mind was just too busy. Although his body was exhausted, his mind wouldn't let him sleep. So he pushed on. Hour after hour. Watching the miles go by, and thinking.

Just after 4 a.m. Central Time, Nick pulled into his driveway in Destin, opened the garage door and pulled the Hellcat inside. As he shut off the engine, he realized that what he had just done was automatic. He hadn't even thought about it. He pressed the correct button and assumed the garage door would open. He had consciously forgotten that he had programmed the garage door opener code into the console controls of the Hellcat, but subconsciously, he remembered.

Nick climbed out, went to the door leading into the house, pressed the correct code on the security system pad and realized that he had just done the same thing again. He had entered the code so many times that it was reflex. Purely muscle memory. It suddenly dawned on him that, just like Dr. Wright had predicted, he was just fine. His memory was working just like everyone else's memory works.

Nick walked into his bedroom, laid down on his bed, fell asleep immediately and slept soundly. When he woke up, it was light outside. He looked at his watch - 9:15. Although he had gotten less than five hours sleep, he felt rested and refreshed. He left his bedroom and walked through the kitchen, stopped briefly to look in the refrigerator out of habit, shut it, then walked to the sliding glass doors leading to the backyard, opened them, and stepped out onto the patio.

The morning sun was shining brilliantly in the clear blue sky and he squinted. There was a light breeze blowing on-shore from the Gulf. Seagulls called noisily in the distance. He took in a deep breath. The salt air filled his lungs and his senses.

A pelican, perched on the top of a corner piling of his dock, squawked as it leaped into the air, then gracefully swooped down to within inches of the surface of the bayou and glided out of sight.

Nick was home. It seemed like he had been gone for years, yet it was just as he remembered. The pool was sparkling clean. Even the grass hadn't grown. Which meant that Tim, his buddy and fellow SEAL, had done exactly what he had promised and kept Nick's place, "Ship-shape and Bristol fashion," as Tim put it, which was an old British Navy term meaning 'in good order and efficiently arranged.' That was Tim.

Nick couldn't resist diving in the pool. He swam a few laps, then climbed out and walked along the wooden planked dock to his boat. The 35 foot Insetta High-Performance Fishing Catamaran, with twin Tohatsu 250 HP V-6's on the back, sat comfortably in her slip. She was bright white with yellow trim. Nick had christened her, 'Bluewater Runner.' As he looked at her, he realized how much he missed partying at Crab Island and fishing offshore.

Then he spotted an ice chest in the boat near the stern. *That shouldn't be there,* he thought, and climbed into the boat, intending to rinse it out on the dock and then sit it up-side-down to dry, but when he opened the lid, he found a partially thawed block of ice and almost a dozen ice-cold bottles of Dos Equis Lager Especial.

"Well now, that's a pleasant surprise." He smiled and said, "Thank you, Tim!"

He grabbed a bottle, popped off the cap with the bottle opener built into the inside of the lid, then closed it and took a long swig.

"Dos for breakfast. Man that's good!"

Then he leaned back in one of the two fishing chairs, propped his feet on the stern, and took another swig of the cold beer.

"Now this is livin'," Nick said.

"Livin' my ass!" a loud voice spoke from toward the bow. "Draw ye broadswords mateys, we gots ourselves a stowaway and he's stealin' all our damn beer!"

Nick jumped up from his chair and met Tim as he stepped down into the boat. They hugged as Nick said, "Man it's good to see you!"

"It's good to see you, too, buddy! When did you get in?"

"Early this morning. Got some shuteye and then I found your stash and decided to have some breakfast."

Nick grabbed Tim a beer, popped the cap, handed it to him, and said, "Have a seat!"

"It's really good to see you, Nick. I was beginning to wonder if you were coming back or not. I was thinking maybe you found a sweet little thing out there in Northern California and decided to stay."

Nick took a long drink, then gave Tim a contemplative look and said, "You have no idea, old friend, you have no idea."

"Well, you arrived a day late, but also, at just the right moment," Tim announced.

"Really? How's that?" Nick asked.

"You won't believe this. We fished the Oriskany night before last. Jack, Dave and I. And, believe it or not, our ladies went along!"

"You're kidding!"

"I kid you not. And we loaded up. We have no idea what happened. We started just before midnight. We were using squid and shrimp. Multiple hooks. Fishing near the bottom. Just catching a few sand bass, and the like. Then, around 1:30, suddenly the triggerfish lit us up. Every line in the water had one or two on. We were fighting our rigs and trying to help the girls bring in theirs. For the next hour or so, we barely had time to keep our lines in the water. When the bite finally stopped, we had ten triggers and not a one was less than five pounds."

"Come on now, you're bullshittin' me!" Nick replied.

"If I'm lyin', I'm dyin'. We also got two nice red snappers. A 20 pounder and another about 18 pounds. We filleted them all here and set aside what we planned to cook tonight. Jack put them in his beer fridge and this morning, he and Allie are vacuum sealing the rest for the freezer. Dave and Susan are helping. We have enough for a bunch more fish feasts."

"Well dang, I hate I missed that."

"Me too. But you're just in time for the feast of all feasts. Julie is at home right now making potato salad and preparing to make her world-famous green salad. We're all meeting at Dave and Susan's this afternoon and cooking. There will be broiled red snapper, fried triggerfish and blackened triggerfish. Baked potatoes. Cole slaw, baked beans, and, of course, my famous Cajun hush puppies. It will be the 'feast de resistance' of all time! And of course, with your impeccable timing, what can I say? Everyone will be thrilled to see you."

"You're makin' me hungry just talkin' about it," Nick said and took another swig of his beer.

"Okay. I was actually just coming by to get my ice chest." Tim admitted. "And here I find you stealing my beer. Now, what about the Northern California project? What do I have no idea about?"

"I was afraid you were gonna get back to that. I was thinkin' I should wait 'til tonight and just tell the tale once to everyone. But then, I don't want to dominate the evening of frivolity and fish feasting with my drama. So…"

Nick reached into the ice chest and retrieved another beer, sat back in his chair, and began. "It all started some months ago on I-10 at Texas Exit 192…

About an hour later, Nick finished his story with, "…then I left Brownsville and here I am."

"Un-frigging-believable!" Tim exclaimed. "And you're okay? Wings level? Squared and balanced?"

"I think so. I'm just not sure where I go from here. I think it's just one day at a time, you know? Speakin' of flyin', I'd really like to get up in the rare air and log some pilot in command time. You up for a run down to the Keys? Maybe bring back some live lobster?"

"Julie's been hinting at some honey dos that I've been putting off. If I can figure a way to sneak away for a few days I'm in."

"Okay, just let me know."

"By the way, speaking of honey, Julie and I saw Cindy at the grocery store the other day. She asked about you."

"I'm not ready for Cindy. Actually, I don't think I'll be ready for a relationship anytime soon. Maybe ever."

"Well, it's probably a good idea not to let Julie know that you're back and just show up. If I tell her you're here, sure as hell she'll invite Cindy. She loves to play matchmaker."

"Thanks, I'll talk with Julie tonight and explain."

Nick returned home from the fish feast, got a good night's sleep, and the next day, got up early, unpacked, and began settling in. He wanted to make his place feel even more like home. He called his boss and explained what had happened, requested that his leave of absence be extended for at least twelve months. His boss advised Nick that he qualified for extended sick leave if he chose. Nick refused and continue his leave of absence.

Chapter 14 Trouble

Over the next few weeks Nick led a life of leisure, spending time with his friends. Fishing and flying, doing repairs and upkeep on his Destin bayou home. He also flew up to Atlanta for a check-up at Shephard Center.

One day, one of Nick's neighbors saw him working outside and came over for a visit. He was an elderly gentleman, introducing himself as Bob, the head of Neighborhood Watch for their community.

Bob told Nick that he had been seeing several strange vehicles cruising slowly up and down their street, and going even slower by his house. He complained that most of the residents drove much too fast and that he had been reporting their tag numbers and vehicle descriptions to the local police. But the unfamiliar vehicles had tag numbers that didn't belong to any of the residents on their street. Since these vehicles, three in all, didn't belong and were exhibiting suspicious behavior by traveling slow each time he saw them, Bob felt that he should warn everyone in the neighborhood to be on the alert, be aware, and keep their homes and property secure.

Nick thanked Bob, and reassured him that he was very careful with home security. As Nick watched Bob walking back toward his house, he called to Bob and said, "Oh, by the way, nice to meet you."

"Same here Nick" Bob replied.

Suddenly Nick felt like an idiot. Bob was doing his job. And he was doing it very well. Bob had total situational awareness, something that had been driven into Nick's brain during SEAL training. Situational awareness had kept him and his team alive in Afghanistan until they failed to spot the roadside bomb that exploded beneath their Humvee.

And Nick had become lax. He was so self-involved with his life, feeling sorry for himself, and living the life of a spoiled and entitled fool that he had almost forgotten who he was.

Nick got busy installing security cameras, motion sensors and motion lights covering his house, property and his boat. He also started using some of that situational awareness that he had so carelessly disregarded. Twice during the ensuing week Nick spotted the vehicles that Bob had voiced concern about. A search of the tag numbers indicated they were rental cars, and that fact gave Nick a bad feeling. There was a very low probability that every member of the Serpiente cartel had been arrested. And even if that had happened, certainly some would be released for lack of evidence or other legal manipulations. Certainly some of those criminals would want revenge. Nick regretted his bad judgement, and wondered if his mistake might lead to something very serious.

One afternoon, Nick decided he would start preparing his supper, but when he looked in the refrigerator, he discovered a grocery run was needed. A short time later he was pushing his grocery cart around the store when a familiar voice from behind him said, "Nick? Is that you?!" which caused him to turn around.

Before he could react, a girl named Cindy said, "I thought it was you!" and gave him a big hug, then stood on her tiptoes and kissed him very tenderly on the lips.

"It's wonderful to see you! I heard you were back home."

"Great to see you too, Cindy."

She was very well made and strikingly beautiful, with light-brown eyes and medium-length straight, brown hair, wearing a low cut, bright yellow sleeveless summer dress with a revealing hemline cut well above her knees.

Nick commented to his buddies more than once that she could make the Pope want to take a second look.

Cindy continued talking but Nick wasn't listening. He was distracted by a memory of her at a party several years previous. She had cajoled him into attending a birthday party for a coworker, who happened to be gay. When she and Nick arrived, Cindy went directly to her friend, standing with his partner, expressed her birthday wishes, and then she gave him a big hug and a very tender kiss, much like the kiss that Nick had just received.

Cindy's friend replied with gracious thank-yous, continued hugging her, then kissed her again, and said something that Nick would never forget: "Honey, you are the only woman that has ever made me want to reconsider my life choices."

The scowl on his partner's face was priceless.

Nick's attention returned to the present-day Cindy, and they talked for a few minutes more, their discussion ending when Nick, against his better judgement, invited Cindy back to his house to have supper with him.

Nick pulled into his garage, with Cindy pulling onto his driveway right behind him. He quickly climbed out, paused for a second, then walked to her car and opened the door to help her climb out. As he closed her door, he asked, "Do you smell gasoline?"

"What?" She replied with a curious expression.

"Gasoline. I smell gasoline and it's really strong too."

"Oh yeah, now that you mention it, I smell it, too. And it is really strong."

It was late afternoon, but dark enough that Nick's motion-activated securing lights above the garage had turned on. Those, together with the lights from inside his garage lit up the driveway and sidewalk leading to the front door.

Nick looked down and exclaimed, "Holy crap!"

The source of the smell was a large puddle of gasoline in front of the garage door, some had flowed underneath the garage door and into the garage. Nick saw his tire tracks leading into the garage from driving through the puddle. It almost completely covered the driveway adjacent to the garage, as well as the sidewalk leading to the front door.

He grabbed Cindy's arm, led her across the lawn and far out of danger, and asked her to call 911. He then ran to his garden hose, turned on the water and began washing the gasoline out of the garage and off of the sidewalk and driveway toward the street.

The first responders arrived within minutes and cleaned up the fuel spill. The fire chief arrived just after the fire truck and did an investigation.

"You two are very fortunate," The chief said, talking to Nick and Cindy. "If either of your cars had ignited the gasoline, there were so many fumes, and such a large quantity of gasoline – I estimate at least five gallons – it's very unlikely that either of you would have survived."

"Oh my God!" Cindy exclaimed.

The chief continued, "The rule of thumb is one gallon of gasoline, mixed with a sufficient quantity of air, has the explosive force of one stick of dynamite. There is no wind right now, so the gasoline fumes, created as gasoline evaporates, would have been hovering over the spill. That's why the smell was so strong when you arrived. Using the rule of thumb that I mentioned, the spill had the potential of an explosive force of four to five sticks of dynamite. With the garage door open, and fumes inside the garage, not only would both of you have been killed, but the house would have been severely damaged, or destroyed, by the explosion and resulting fire. We may have been able to save part of the house."

"Wow!" Nick said in amazement. He looked at Cindy and said, "God was looking out for us."

"He certainly was." The chief agreed, then asked, "Do you have any idea who might be responsible for this?"

"Not really," Nick replied.

"I see that you have security cameras," The chief commented.

"As a matter of fact, I do," Nick said. "Come in and we'll have a look. I can bring the security video up on my phone, but my laptop will provide a better view."

Nick, Cindy and the chief went inside and viewed the security video. The results were disappointing. The perpetrator wore nondescript clothes, and a baseball cap pulled low to cover his eyes. He skirted the edge of the camera's field of view, poured out the gasoline quickly and then returned the way he came.

"He had studied the positioning of your cameras," The chief suggested. "And although he skillfully avoided showing his face, he boldly committed the crime in broad daylight. He could have simply tossed a match as he skulked away. Which might have backfired – no pun intended – and killed himself. He could have left a timed piezoelectric igniter, or simply waited until you pulled into your garage, then drove by and fired a flare. But instead, he simply made a statement; 'I could have killed you, but I didn't'."

The chief stood up and said, "I've given you enough to think about. Just one more suggestion. You're obviously being stalked by a very dangerous person, or persons. If I were you, I'd keep my head on a swivel."

Nick walked to the door with the chief, thanked him and bid him goodnight. Then he returned to his computer to shut it down. Cindy was watching the video for the countless time. She looked up at him with a very concerned expression and said, "This guy is threatening to kill you!"

"Looks that way."

"We could've both been burned alive!" She exclaimed.

Nick reached down and caressed her cheek, then pulled her against him and said, "I'm sorry for puttin' you in danger. That scares me. And I feel foolish for lettin' it happen."

Cindy stood up and looked him in the eyes. "Let it happen? How could you possibly have let it happen? Did you know a strange guy was planning to pour gasoline all over your driveway before you went to buy groceries?!"

"Well, no."

"Then how did you let it happen?"

"I've just been walkin' around here with my head up my ass!"

"Could you please explain what you mean by that? I think there's much more to your self-criticism."

Nick took a deep breath and sighed. "As usual, your intuitive mind sees right through me. Come sit with me on the sofa and get comfortable. It's a long story…"

Cindy sat enthralled, listening to every word as Nick related the story. When he finished, she sat back and said, "My goodness! That could be made into a movie."

"Sometimes it almost seems like fiction. Except that my ears are still ringin' from that missile blast."

Then she leaned closer, tenderly touched his face and said, "I also think that I've lost you to a beautiful Cherokee girl."

"I'm not lost, I just don't know where I am at the moment."

Cindy kissed him passionately. Then she said, "Before we have dessert… I have had the strangest evening maybe ever. And I'm starving. Beauchamp's should still be open…"

"I get the hint. You don't have to hit me over the head with a platter of Oyster's Beauchamp and a pitcher of ice-cold draft beer."

"Sounds perfect," She purred.

Cindy stayed the night. They had dessert and slept late. She called in sick and stayed the next day. Nick took her for a short cruise into the Gulf on Bluewater Runner, then returned inshore and anchored at Crab Island to swim and soak up some sun.

Late that afternoon they relaxed on his dock, having icy drinks and watching the golden sun drop through a sky-blue-pink sky and disappear into the Gulf. The air was still and as the fading rays of the sun transformed the high clouds into a glowing red fire, the bayou looked as though it had become orange glass.

"That sunset is breathtaking," Cindy said.

Nick looked over at her and said, "Thanks for staying."

"You needed company," she replied. "Not necessarily my company, but I needed to be with you."

"Considering what's been goin' on, I'm not exactly a good choice for company."

Cindy reached out and caressed his shoulder. "Nick, I feel safer with you than anyone I know."

He put his hand on hers. Then she added, "I've missed you."

Cindy stayed that night, too. They had desert again.

The next morning Cindy woke early, and while Nick slept, she brought coffee and donuts from The Donut Hole. They watched the sunrise as they had breakfast together on the patio.

Then she kissed him goodbye, saying, "Take care of you," and rush off to work.

Nick continued to relax on the patio, enjoying his coffee and thinking. He was glad that Cindy had stayed. He needed her affection and her passion. Yet, he also felt that he had been unfaithful to Walela.

He fell asleep and slept until mid-morning when a crack of thunder interrupted his nap. Then it began to rain. Nick loved the sound of rain. It soothed his mind and gave him a secure feeling, being in a dry and comfortable place watching the rain fall.

But this was springtime in Florida. Costal thundershowers tend to produce a lot of rain in a very short period. And this was one of those thundershowers. Nick was soon chased inside by the blowing rain. Then it began to rain so hard that it almost seemed like it was hailing. The kind of hard rain that you might think could beat the hair off of a horse's back.

He was reminded of a joke his grandfather told about Texas thundershowers. Nick grew up on a small ranch near San Angelo. His father was an investment banker in the oil industry. His mother was a teacher. He spent a lot of time with his paternal grandfather, who owned a much larger ranch adjacent to his parent's ranch. Nick loved his grandfather and loved to hear him tell jokes. Once, when it was raining fairly hard, his grandfather said, "Aw heck, this ain't nothin'. One time it was rainin' so hard that it filled the bed of my pickup truck plum full of water. But what snatched the skin off the steer wus I'd done fergot and left the dang tailgate down."

Nick sat on his sofa and watched the thundershower raging outside. He suddenly missed his Hummingbird terribly. He needed her curled up beside him. She liked to watch the rain, too.

Chapter 15 Reunion

Several days later, while Nick was sleeping in the early morning hours, a motion sensor triggered an alarm on his phone, waking him up. He strapped on his shoulder holster carrying his Glock 19. Then he grabbed his knife of choice, the K-Bar that he carried while on active duty, and silently slipped downstairs and out the back door.

Once outside, he silently moved in the direction of the motion sensor's location. He discovered the perpetrator, dressed in black sweats and a black hoodie, attempting to defeat the lock on the side door into the garage. Little did the guy know, Nick had manually bolted the door from the inside.

The guy saw Nick, drew his knife and attacked. Nick drew his knife and countered. He side-stepped the guy's charge and kicked him into the wall, causing him to drop his knife. The guy drew his pistol, Nick grabbed the guy's wrist and lifted it just as he fired. With his other hand he sank the K-Kar into his opponent's chest. The man went limp and dropped to his knees as Nick, continuing to hold his wrist, pulled the gun out of his hand.

He grabbed at Nick with his other arm as he fell over on his side. Nick kneeled down, looked the guy in the face and asked, "Who sent you?"

He didn't answer.

Seeing that he had Hispanic features, Nick asked again in Spanish, "¿Quién te envió?"

The guy looked up at Nick and, in English, said, "Fuck you. You're all dead."

Then he died.

On the street, the remaining two occupants of a strange car parkcd ncar Nick's house heard the gunshot immediately exited the car and were moving slowly and quietly toward the house.

Nick ducked into a row of tall oleander that served as a fence between his house and the house next door. As the second and third man carefully moved along the row of oleander, the camera on the corner of the house turned on and activated a security light. The second man shot out the light and dashed toward the one lying on the ground.

The third man spun around, checking for movement behind him, then began moving forward again towards his partner, who was bending down to check for life in his dead companion. As the third man moved passed where Nick was hiding, Nick stepped out, grabbed his left arm and simultaneously sank his K-Bar to the hilt in his right kidney. The second man heard his companion groan and turned to look as Nick fired two rounds from the pistol, still in the man's hand. The second man slumped forward as Nick extracted his knife and let the third man's limp body fall to the ground. Nick then went back inside, picked up his cell phone and dialed 911.

It was bright daylight before the Sheriff's department finished their investigation. Just as the deputies drove away, the fire chief drove up, got out and rang the doorbell.

Nick answered the door. "Oh hello, Chief. Come on in."

"I hope I'm not bothering you. I'm sure you've had enough of local officials by now. But I heard the call, recognized your address, and thought I'd stop by to check on you."

"Thanks for thinking of me, Chief. Can I pour you a cup of coffee? This is about the fifth pot I've brewed this morning."

The chief laughed. "After all that work, I can hardly refuse."

Nick poured him a cup and they sat down at the dining table.

"I could've rushed right over," the Chief began, "but I hung back. I didn't want to get in the way of the investigators. What was their conclusion?"

"Justified. The intent was obvious."

"Honestly, after the fuel spill, I've been expecting to respond to a dwelling fire with fatalities."

Nick looked down at this cup and said, "Just before he died, the first one that I killed said, 'you're all dead'."

"You live alone here, correct?"

"Yes, sir."

"Who else was he referring to? And while I'm asking, unless it's none of my business, why is a bunch of cartel thugs after you?"

"Sir, I think you know more than you're letting on."

"All three of the dead guys are suspected members of a gang tied to the California Cartel. They've been smuggling crystal meth and fentanyl into the Emerald Coast for over a year. They're also suspected of human trafficking."

"I crossed the Serpiente Cartel in south Texas a few months ago and rescued my sister-in-law and nine other kidnapped teenage girls. I had help – my wife and her cousin - the 'others' that he was referrin' to. They're in Oklahoma right now."

"Lieutenant Commander, I've also done some research in your direction. You have a very impressive history. Since you have family out west that are also in danger. I think you need to circle the wagons."

"Yes, sir, you're right. I knew it the instant that punk said it. They're out for revenge. I'm headin' out in the mornin'."

"We all know they're ruthless, so keep your head on a swivel."

"I will, sir."

"I'll take my leave now. I think you'll be busy securing your place before you head out."

The chief stood up, shook Nick's hand and said, "It has been an honor to meet you, Nick. Godspeed."

"Thank you, sir."

After the chief left, Nick felt that he should call Walela, but he wasn't sure what he would say, so he sent a text instead: *"Danger may be close. Watch your back. Don't trust anyone. Keep yourself, Noya, and Tala safe. Hope you're well. More later."*

She replied, *"Do not make it too 'later'."*

The following morning, Nick headed north on US-331, then west on I-10, destination Muskogee, Oklahoma. His route took him through Mobile, Gulfport, Slidell, Baton Rouge, and on to Lafayette where he turned northwest on I-49.

He stopped for gas and food in Lafayette. Up to this point in his trip, Nick was fairly certain that he wasn't being followed. But just after he stopped, he spotted two characters that seemed out of place. He could either continue his trip, taking his chances that they would follow and try to either kill him or kidnap him further on down the road, or he could give them the opportunity to execute their plans immediately. He decided on the latter.

It was already dark, so he figured they might be more likely to try something. He fueled up, ate, and then moved his Hellcat to a poorly lit area in the back of the parking lot and waited.

Very soon, they pulled their car behind him and both got out. One approached his driver's door and tapped on the window. The other approached his passenger door. Nick rolled his window down slightly to ask what the guy wanted, but all he did was point a pistol at Nick and motion for him to get out.

Nick slowly opened the door, stood up, and then slammed the door against the guy, causing him to lose his grip on his gun. Nick grabbed it, spun the barrel around against his chest and fired. With a muted bang the guy collapsed at his feet. Nick quickly dropped down out of view of the guy on the passenger side. The guy moved around the rear of his car, trying to get a clear field of fire. But as he came into view, Nick threw his knife and impaled the guy in the chest. He grabbed at the knife as he fell dead on the ground.

Nick stood up and looked around to see if anyone saw the commotion. Seeing no one, he reached down and retrieved his knife, wiped the blood off of the blade on the guy's shirt, wiped his fingerprints off of the gun, then got back in his Hellcat and drove away.

The next point on his trip was Alexandria, then on through Shreveport, and to Texarkana. He hadn't spotted anyone following him, so there he headed north on Highway 59/71 to Cove, Oklahoma on the Choctaw Nation, then northwest on US Highway 259, to Kenta, then north on the Cherokee Nation and finally to Muskogee.

The Bell's lived north of Muskogee, near the Arkansas River. He was confident that Walela would be there because she flew to Oklahoma. Nick realized during his trip that he should alert her family because they could also be in danger. He was especially concerned about Tala, because the cartel might try to kidnap her again, or kill her just to make a point.

It was mid-morning when Nick pulled up and stopped by the mailbox. Located in a sparsely-populated rural community, the Bell's home was a large, ranch-style house with an elevated floor plan due to being within the flood plane of the Arkansas River.

Horses, cattle, sheep, and goats grazed in fenced green pastures on either side of the driveway. The house was set in a cluster of large shade trees. Beyond the house there was a large garden and a partially enclosed pole barn with a farm tractor parked inside.

Nick drove slowly up the driveway and parked behind Walela's Raptor, still uncertain what he would say to her.

"Well, she's here," He said to himself and was suddenly not all that thrilled about walking up and knocking on the door. Then three dogs came running and barking from the back of the house and Nick realized that, like it or not, his arrival had been announced.

He thought for only a moment before deciding to open the door instead of waiting for someone to come and rescue him from the dogs, now wagging tails, standing on their hind legs with front paws on his door, barking at him through the window. They didn't act vicious, but he figured getting dog bit might garner some sympathy in case of feelings of animosity toward him. After all, he had essentially kicked Walela out of his life.

Much to Nick's relief, the dogs were all happy to see him and had just been anxious for him to get out and pet them. The dogs escorted him to the door and he rang the bell. He patiently waited. The dogs were looking at him and then the door, as if he had been elected to open it and let them inside.

Suddenly the front door opened and there stood Walela, looking at Nick through the glass storm door. She gasped, obviously shocked to see him, and covered her mouth with both of her hands.

"Hi," Nick managed to utter.

Walela just stood there, eyes wide, hands still covering her mouth.

"I think the dogs want in," Nick observed and managed a slight smile.

The dogs responded by getting more excited.

"Oh!" She replied as she suddenly regained her composure. "I'm sorry! Please, come in."

Nick started to open the storm door and the dogs crowded in, trying to push their way past Nick.

"Not you!" She scolded. "Go play!" And pointed toward the front yard.

The dogs backed away. Nick opened the door and stepped inside.

They stood, facing each other. Walela's hair was done into two long pigtails. She was wearing a large pink nightshirt with a picture of an enraged grizzly baring claws and teeth with the words, "hug me" underneath.

"You look great," Nick observed.

"So do you," She replied, trying to force a smile.

"Is that a warning, or an order?" Nick asked, pointing to her shirt.

She looked down, stretched the shirt out, as if she needed to see what was printed on it.

"Oh this," She chuckled. "I, ah… didn't feel like getting dressed…"

"I'm thinkin' bear hug." Nick said, then grabbed her tightly and lifted her off the floor.

Walela put her arms around his neck. Then she buried her face on his shoulder, began to cry and whispered, "Oh Nick! I've missed you so much!"

He hugged her for a long moment, then eased her back down so that her bare feet touched the floor, wiped the tears from her eyes and said, "I've missed you too, Hummingbird."

Then he tenderly kissed her, long and deep.

She seemed to wilt in his arms. Then she wrapped her arms around him and whispered, "I was so afraid that I would never taste your kisses again."

"I hope you know that I'm still so mad at you that I could strangle you," Nick announced.

Walela looked at him with the expression of a scolded puppy. "Nick, I am so ashamed of what I did to you. It seems almost insane that I came up with such a cruel plan."

"Sweetheart, I understand your motive. You were actin' in desperation. But all you had to do was ask. What you failed to realize, I was captivated by you from the moment that I first saw you. Heck, after our first date, if you had asked me to jump off a cliff, I would've started tryin' to figure out how to do it and survive so that I could ask you out again."

"You remember," She stated the obvious.

"Yep."

She sighed deeply. "I've been such a fool!"

"You're not a fool, just fool*ish.* But that's understandable. You're a female. Foolish plottin' and schemin' is part of your DNA."

Walela gave Nick an incredulous look. "I'm not sure I like that!"

Nick looked at her sternly and replied, "Just own it and try to avoid givin' in to it."

She looked at him thoughtfully, sighed and said, "I can live with that."

"Good," Nick replied. "Then we're makin' progress."

"Well, I'm sure you didn't drive all this way just to stand at Mom's front door and kiss me." Walela took his hand and pulled him toward the kitchen.

"Mom is in the garden gathering veggies for dinner, and I'm about to put a roast in the oven. Would you like a cup of coffee?"

"That sounds good," Nick replied.

She poured his coffee, served him a chocolate muffin and got one for herself.

Presently Walela's mother came in the back door, which opened into a small mud room, then through that door, which was open, into the kitchen. She was carrying a straw basket filled with vegetables. She didn't notice Nick at first, sat the basket on the kitchen counter beside the sink and turned to Walela, started to speak, but stopped short when she spotted Nick. He stood up from the table.

"Nick, this is my mom, Aiyana. Her name means 'Eternal Blossom'."

"Mom, this is Nick."

Nick went to her and offered his hand.

She shook his hand and said, "I'm so pleased to meet you, Nick. Walela has told us so much about you."

"It's an honor to meet you, missus Bell."

"Please, just call me Mom. Everyone does. And make yourself at home. Finish your coffee. I have to wash these vegetables."

She turned and walked toward the sink. As Aiyana brushed passed Walela, she pinched her on the cheek and whispered, "Ulilohi!" (Meaning 'handsome').

Walela blushed, smiled and cut her eyes toward Nick.

Nick gave her a curious look.

She mouthed the words, "I'll tell you later."

As Aiyana returned to her task at the sink, she looked over at Nick and asked, "Have you just driven up from Florida?"

"Yes ma'am, I decided to drive as straight northwest as I could. I wanted to drive across the Nations."

"Oh, how nice! It's been a long time since I've been south. My husband used to hunt there. We would take the kids and camp on Lake Eufaula."

"Yes!" Walela added, "We had so much fun! Dad taught us how to hunt and fish. We cooked over an open fire and learned how to make a proper camp. We swam in the lake. I wish we could do that again."

"Me too, Hummingbird. Those were good days. Very good days."

Hearing Aiyana call her 'Hummingbird,' Nick looked at Walela in surprise.

Walela beamed a wide, happy smile.

The three talked the day away as Walela and her mother continued to prepare supper, stopping only briefly to eat lunch. Although, Walela switched from coffee to wine, then snacked on muffins and veggies through the morning and afternoon, finishing most of a bottle of wine by herself.

Later that day, in the late afternoon, Walela's father returned home from work. She met him as he came in the back door.

"Hello, my father," she said as she kissed him on the cheek.

"Hello Walela," he replied, then went to Aiyana, kissed her and said, "Hello, my love."

Then Walela went to her father, took him by the arm and pulled him to where Nick was standing beside the dining table.

"Father, this is Nick."

"Nick, this is my father, Danuwoa. His name means, 'The Warrior'."

Danuwoa reached out and shook Nick's hand, "I'm pleased to meet you, young man."

"Sir, I'm honored," Nick replied.

"Walela is being so formal, calling me 'Father'." He said, giving her a curious look. "Please, call me Dad. Everyone does. When did you get in, Nick?"

"Midmornin' today."

"I hope you had an uneventful trip."

"It was… interesting."

Walela listened and snacked on the roast as she cut it up and prepared it for supper.

"He came up from the south, across the Nations." Aiyana added.

"Yes, it's beautiful country," Nick observed.

"We used to camp, hunt, and fish there. On Lake Eufaula," Danuwoa recalled.

"We were talking about that earlier," Aiyana said, then announced, "Everyone wash up! Dinner is ready."

Chapter 16 Bad News and Good News

After everyone had finished eating, before anyone left the table, Nick thanked Aiyana and Walela for the delicious meal and then said, "Since we're all together, I think this is a good time to explain why I'm here."

Walela had sensed there was more to his visit than just trying repair their relationship, and said, "It has something to do with the text that you sent, doesn't it?"

"Actually, it has everything to do with that text."

"What text?" Danuwoa asked.

"I sent a warning. You're all in danger. Walela didn't say anything because she knows me well enough to realize that message was for her eyes only."

"How are we in danger?" Aiyana asked.

"Someone wants revenge for the takedown of the Serpiente in Matamoros. I don't know if it's some of the cartel that the Mexican Federal Police didn't catch, or if it's some of their friends that feel they owe the Serpiente. I've had an encounter with thugs connected to the California Cartel. I don't know exactly what they're up to. They first poured five gallons of gasoline all over my driveway and sidewalk, but didn't ignite it. They could have, usin' a simple flare gun, when I was standin' right in the middle of the puddle, as the fire chief pointed out.

"Maybe they thought it would ignite when I came back from the grocery store and parked in my garage. But if that was their plan, it wasn't a very good one. If gasoline spills on concrete were easily ignited by vehicles, we'd have fires at service stations almost every day. And if they were just tryin' to intimidate me, that didn't work either. All it did was piss me off because my garage smelled like gasoline and the gas killed part of my front lawn.

"But the next attempt, just a few days ago, was more serious. My security system alerted me. I found a guy tryin' to break in to my garage. He attacked me. I killed him. But before he died, he said,

'You're all dead'. Not, 'you're dead', but 'you're *all* dead'. He had two accomplices. I killed both. After that I sent Walela the text. And then headed here the next day.

"The first night I was attacked by two more. I eliminated them and haven't seen anyone else followin' me. I wouldn't have led them here. I'm not certain if their intention was to kill me or just kidnap me. The thing is, they're deadly serious and we can only assume that they intend to kill or kidnap all of us, because the guy said we're 'all dead'. That fits the cartel's typical behavior, killing their enemies along with their families."

"How could they know about us here in Oklahoma?" Danuwoa asked.

"We gained some notoriety while we were in the hospital in Brownsville. The media interviewed some of the girls we rescued. I didn't read any of the stories, but names may have been released. ICE should have kept a lid on that, but probably didn't."

"I'll call Noya now," Walela said as she picked up her smartphone.

"Where is she?" Nick asked.

"She's at the cabin taking care of Sprocket and the livestock."

"And Tala?"

"She's with Noya, taking a break from her therapy."

Nick looked at Danuwoa. "Dad, you can take care of Mom. I need to head to Balmorhea."

"I'm going with you!" Walela announced while she was still on the phone talking to Noya.

"Yes, Noya, that was Nick," she replied, continuing her phone conversation…

"Yes, we're coming there. Probably leave in the morning."

"How's Tala? That's great! It's doing her good to spend some quality time with you."

"No, Nick isn't mad," Walela lied.

"No, he hasn't mentioned killing you, not even once. He has mentioned something about strangling me. No, not you. Yes, I'm sure."

"Don't be silly. You can't hide from him! Besides, where would you go?"

"The Caverns of Sonora? That's ridiculous."

"Yes, it's beautiful down there. And the climate is perfect. But they won't let you hide in the caves."

"They would find you when you came out to use the bathroom."

"Okay, Noya, you can shut up. You're just being gross. Nick isn't going to kill you. We'll be there late tomorrow afternoon. Love you, too."

"What was all that about me killing Noya?" Nick asked.

"She thinks that you're so mad at her that you're going to kill her."

"Well, I am mad, but not that mad."

"I told her that you're not mad."

Nick looked at Walela. "I'm sure that Noya is well aware that you'll lie when it suits you."

She turned and walked away, saying, "That's why she didn't believe me when I said you're not mad at her."

After things had settled down from Nick's announcement, everyone was sitting in the living room having desert and discussing plans for the upcoming days. Mom suddenly asked Walela to walk outside with her.

"Were you planning on allowing Nick to sleep in your room tonight?"

"Well, yes ma'am, I was."

"Do I need to remind you that you two are not actually married?"

"Oh, Mom!" Walela rolled her eyes. "We lived together for months."

"That doesn't make it right."

"I know. But, Mom, I love him. And I believe he loves me."

Aiyana placed her hands on Walela's cheeks, looked into her eyes and stated, "You're carrying his child."

Tears formed in Walela's eyes. "How did you know?!"

"I began to suspect when you were having morning sickness. Then your appetite increased. How far along are you?"

"Just over twelve weeks."

"You're eating for two now," Aiyana observed. "Your appetite will be a bit crazy for a while. But you're drinking too much wine. That needs to stop. Now. Drink water."

"Yes, Mom, you're right."

She placed her hand on Walela's belly and said, "You'll be showing soon."

Then Aiyana hugged her, kissed her cheek and said, "Aye, my sweet Hummingbird. You've gone and made me a grandmother again. Your brothers will be happy that they are not the only ones giving us grandchildren, and your sister will be thrilled."

Just as Walela and Aiyana came back inside, Nick stood up and said, "I need to get my bag out of the wagon."

"Put your stuff in my room," Walela commanded.

Everyone looked at her in surprise.

"What?!" She asked innocently.

There was no more discussion. When Nick brought his bag to her room, she was waiting for him.

"I'm not sure your folks are all that thrilled about me sleeping with you." Nick said, then added, "I'm a bit unsure, too."

"Why?" She asked innocently as she slipped her arms around his waist and looked up at him.

"It just feels… strange I guess. I mean, I just met your folks. We're under their roof."

"Well, technically, they still believe the old ways, so it's actually Mom's roof," Walela pointed out.

"That doesn't exactly make me feel any better about this," Nick confessed.

She couldn't wait any longer.

"Nick, I'm pregnant with your baby."

His expression froze.

"Nick? Did you hear what I just said?"

She waved her hand in front of his eyes. He didn't blink.

"Hello? Are you in there?"

Suddenly he swept her up in his arms. She squealed, he kissed her, and then gently laid her on the bed. Then he climbed on top of her, placed his hands on either side of her at arm's length and asked, "We're havin' a baby? Really?"

"Look, I know I've lied to you a zillion times during the past six months, but I would never lie to you about *this!* Yes! I'm having your baby. I'm a little more than twelve weeks pregnant."

Nick leaned down to kiss her, being careful not to put any of his body weight on her.

"Hey, big guy, I'm not suddenly made of glass. Kiss me," she ordered, grabbed him around his neck and pulled him down on top of her. They didn't sleep much that night.

The next morning, Nick and Walela departed for Balmorhea. Within an hour, she was curled up on the seat beside him with a pillow and a blanket, sound asleep. Although he didn't say anything to her about it, Nick was not comfortable about Walela going back to Texas with him. He felt that she would be in less danger in Muskogee. But he also knew that she was concerned about Tala. Nick was impressed with how protective her family was of each other. And he wasn't about to interfere with that. Besides, as he looked at her sleeping peacefully, he knew his Hummingbird was safe and secure with him.

Nick and Walela arrived at the cabin in late afternoon. Long shadows were forming as the sun crawled toward the distant horizon. They were greeted by an excited and happy Sprocket, who recognized the sound of Nick's Hellcat before he could see it.

Walela opened the door to pet Sprocket. Just as Nick stepped out, Tala, who had been standing by the pond when they arrived, saw him and came running. Without saying a word, she leaped into his arms, wrapped her legs around his waist, closed her eyes and hugged him as tightly as she could.

"Hello, gunfighter," Nick said.

Walela tenderly rubbed Tala's back and then kissed her on the cheek. Tala turned her face toward Walela, but still didn't speak.

Walela smiled and said, "Hi, little sister."

"Hi," She whispered.

"How are you doing?"

"I'm okay."

"Okay?" Nick interjected. "She is amazing! This little fighter has the heart of a lion and a ferocious wolf rolled into one. She handles a side arm like a true warrior."

Then Tala looked into Nick's eyes, burst into tears and said, "Thank you for saving me!"

Nick held her close and let her cry as Walela consoled her. Then Nick wiped Tala's tears away, looked into her eyes and said, "Okay, first of all, you're welcome. I'm proud to have been a part of your rescue. But I could *not* have done it without your courageous help.

No operation as daring as that happens without teamwork. And you didn't even know that you were part of the team. You just jumped in there, picked up a weapon and started savin' lives. The first life you saved was mine. There is no way I could have driven that van to the border without your help because they would have killed me. You were under direct, withering fire, but you didn't hesitate. You stepped up, returned deadly-accurate fire and risked your life to defeat the enemy. That is the mark of a true warrior. A hero. Young lady, I would trust you to have my back any day."

"Really?"

"Damn straight! And just as soon as I can arrange it, I'm gonna see that you're awarded an honorary SEAL badge."

Tala just stared at Nick.

"She's speechless," Walela observed in amazement. "I did not think that was possible."

Tala cut her eyes toward her sister. "I'm a hero. Just remember that."

Walela kissed her and said, "I'm so proud of you!"

Tala hugged her and said, "Thank you."

Just then, Noya peaked out of the back door.

Sprocket saw her and ran over as if trying to coax her to come outside.

Walela saw her and waved.

"She's been worrying and watching all afternoon," Tala revealed.

Walela called to her, "It is ok, Noya, you can come out."

Nick started walking toward the back door, then Walela and Tala followed. He reached the door, opened it, and hugged Noya.

"You're not mad?" Noya asked.

"I didn't say that."

"Lea said you weren't mad."

"She lied."

Noya scowled at her.

"I'm not mad because you hacked my brain. You had good reason for doin' anything you could possibly do to find and rescue Tala. I would do the same thing."

"Then why are you angry?" Noya asked.

"Because you didn't ask."

"What?" Noya replied vacantly.

"All that you and your beautiful cousin had to do was ask me. I would've helped you in a heartbeat."

"You're kidding," Noya said, giving Walela a mean look.

"Nope," Nick replied.

"I'm so ashamed," Walela confessed.

"You're ashamed?" Noya spoke accusingly to Walela. "You're ashamed? I hacked into this gorgeous man's head and totally screwed up his life! And all we had to do was ask for his help?"

Noya was almost yelling at this point.

"I was fired from a job that I loved because I misused classified government equipment and acted in an unethical manner. I could have been prosecuted and gone to jail! *And all we had to do was ask for his help! This is a frigging nightmare!!*"

"I had no idea that you'd been fired," Nick declared.

"I forgot to tell you," Walela admitted. "She received the news just after Doctor Aberman returned to Atlanta."

"I'm so sorry, Noya," Nick said and hugged her.

"I deserve this," Noya commented dryly. "I screw up your life and you're apologizing to me."

"Noya, you haven't screwed up my life. Do you not see that we, Hummingbird and I, are here together? Certainly, you both schemed a convoluted and overly-complicated way to get a very difficult task accomplished. But everyone involved has to give both of you credit for innovative thinkin'.

"And the best part is, because of how you went about this crazy plot, Hummingbird and I had the most amazing time together here at this cabin. I was already in love with her. You're reprogramming couldn't change that, because it happened in California, almost at the moment Walela and I met. And she had to be part of my new memory.

"Walela fell in love with me right here. That had nothing to do with you either, or anything else, except maybe fate and God's will that brought us together. And thanks to your hacking skills, and the divine hand of God, we were led to save Tala and all the others. We are all blessed to be a part of this adventure."

Noya looked at Nick and confessed, "I don't know what to say."

"And my lover has rendered yet another of my family speechless," Walela declared.

Noya gave her a curious look.

"It happened to me just a few minutes ago," Tala explained.

"Oh," Noya replied.

Then Tala looked at Walela and asked, "So, when Nick rescued me, he introduced himself as my brother-in-law, but when you came home, you told us that you weren't married. So which is it?"

"We're not married," She replied.

"Yet," Nick added, and all three ladies quickly looked at him.

"What?" Nick asked with an innocent look.

"What do you mean, 'what'?" Noya asked. "You said, 'Yet.' Are you saying that you're about to pop the question?"

"I just meant we're not married *yet*."

"Well then, are you engaged?" Tala asked.

"Not yet," Nick replied.

"Well, when then?!" Noya asked impatiently.

"When then what?" Nick replied.

Walela chuckled.

"Are you two messing with us?" Noya asked suspiciously.

"No," Walela replied, smiling.

"Why are you smiling?" Tala asked suspiciously. "What's going on?"

Tala looked at Noya and said, "They're not telling us something."

Then they both looked expectantly at Walela.

She looked at Nick. "Should I?"

He nodded.

"I'm pregnant."

Tala and Noya both screamed and hugged Walela.

"How far along are you?" Noya asked.

"In four days it will be thirteen weeks."

"Are you showing yet?" Tala asked.

"Not yet. Maybe in a couple of weeks."

"I can't wait!" Tala said, excitedly.

"How about let's go celebrate?" Nick suggested.

"Great idea!" Walela replied, "I'm starving."

They all loaded into the Hellcat and headed to the Circle Bar & Saddleback Steakhouse. When it was Walela's turn to order, for her drink, she asked for red wine. Nick cleared his throat and looked at her. She gave him a sheepish look and said, "Cancel the wine, I'll just have water…"

Chapter 17 Circle the Wagons

Months earlier, Bartholomew "Bart" Gris stared at his nearly-empty bottle of tequila sitting on his bar and fidgeted with it. He was doing what he called 'thinkin' drinkin'. Then he took another large swallow.

The bottle had been half-full when he started drinking about an hour ago, right after he received a phone call. The call was from a computer guy, Samson Block. It was bad news. Alphonze "Al" Reale had been found in his bed, shot in the head. Al was Bart's brother in arms. His compadre. Bart trusted Al. They had history. After Gris formed the California Cartel, Reale was the first cartel head to propose an alliance. He could always count on Al to have his back. Now Al was dead. And Bart wanted revenge. He was filled with rage and he wanted revenge.

Gris picked up the tequila bottle and drank one more swallow, then threw it across the room. The bottle hit the wall and shattered. Then he picked up his phone and called one of his lieutenants…

"Mateo, who did this thing?"

"Then find out. I want 'em dead. First I want 'em to sweat. I want 'em to know they're gonna die before I make 'em dead."

"I don't care what it takes. Find 'em!"

Mateo put his phone down. "What the hell does he expect me to do?"

"What's that, boss?" Pedro, Mateo's driver and bodyguard asked.

"Somebody capped Reale. Now the boss wants me to find him. What do I look like? A bloodhound? I don't find people, I move product. This is bullshit!"

"Call the Geek. He can find anything," Pedro suggested without taking his eyes away from the windshield.

"Hey! Now you're thinking," Mateo exclaimed and slapped Pedro on the arm with the back of his hand, "That's why you get the big bucks."

Pedro just rolled his eyes and kept driving.

******

Just after Nick and Walela departed for Texas, Danuwoa and Aiyana called their four sons on a conference call and updated them on the threat to the family. After that, the boys discussed plans. Before the end of the day, each one, their wife and kids were headed to Mom's house. And they were armed to the teeth.

******

Samson Block stared at his phone, expecting a call. It had been only days since he fled Matamoros by hitching a ride with a trucker heading into the US from a farm in central Mexico. He knew someone would call and he dreaded it. He was expecting a call because he had made a call that he regretted as soon as he made it. But Block loved gossip, and he also needed a job. When he received confirmation that his boss had been murdered, he couldn't resist being the first one to break the news to the head of the California Cartel. Block knew they were close. He had done a few favors for Gris at the request of Reale. Maybe Gris would be grateful to receive the bad news from a trusted Serpiente associate.

"Hell, who am I kidding?" He thought. *"I'm just the 'computer guy.' The guy everyone refers to as 'the geek' behind my back."*

"Well, I'm not a geek," Block mumbled to himself, "I'm an IT specialist. A webmaster."

Just then his phone rang. Block cringed, but answered.

"Block."

"Yo, Block, it's Mateo, remember me? I hooked you up a while back to do a favor for my boss?"

"Oh sure, I remember."

"Hey, I'm sorry to hear about Reale. He was solid."

"Thanks, I appreciate that."

"And speaking of that, I'm thinking that we should respond in kind, if you follow my meaning. An eye for an eye. Maybe many eyes for an eye. You feel me?"

"I'm listening," Block replied, and then thought, *"Here it comes."*

"This guy needs to be found. My man says you're the one to do it."

"I'm… humbled. Listen, I've just found myself in the wind. Would you consider…"

"I hear you. Just do your geek magic and we'll see."

"Thank you, sir, I'll do my best."

Block tossed his phone on the dining table in a rundown, ratty little apartment located in a rough neighborhood of Dallas, Texas and cursed.

"Nice move, ex-lax!" He said to himself. "You don't have internet service. You don't even have a damn computer, and you just told an executive member of the California Cartel, 'I'll do my best'! And to top it all, I don't know any names, but I'll bet my left nut it was that guy who threatened to hunt me down and skin me before he killed me."

Then Block realized something – the hostage rescue had attracted a lot of press coverage; radio, TV, newspapers, internet. As sloppy and careless as reporters are about facts and details, one of them had to mention names. It was just a matter of searching, and he could use a computer at the library to do that…

A week later, after exhaustive reading and searching, Block found a story about a hero named Nickolas Conner that rescued ten kidnapped girls. Then he hacked into the Valley Regional Medical Center's patient registry and found that Tala Bell had been in the same hospital room with Nickolas Conner. Since when did hospitals allow males and females with different last names to stay in the same room? She had to be the girl Conner was hunting.

When he hacked into the Southwest Airlines departing passenger manifests, he found that Walela Bell had departed on a Southwest flight to Tulsa, Oklahoma the same day that Nickolas Conner was released from the hospital. He also found records of a Bell family in Muscogee, Oklahoma that had four sons and two daughters. The daughters were named Walela and Tala. A nationwide Amber Alert had been previously issued from the Dallas, Texas area for a suspected kidnapping victim, Tala Bell, and then a recent cancellation of the alert stating that Tala had been found and returned home safe.

Further searching for Nickolas Conner and Walela Bell in Oklahoma and Texas found recent vehicle registrations in Reeves County, Texas and provided an address near Balmorhea. The registration information included the previous address of Nickolas Conner in Destin, Florida.

Block knew he had found them and immediately sent the information to Mateo. He thanked Block and reassured him that he would recommend that Gris put him on the payroll. When Mateo called Gris, he forwarded Block's information and then took credit for finding Reale's killer so quickly. Gris immediately put out the word to find them, bring Conner to him, alive, and kill everyone else.

******

On their way home from the steakhouse, they met a black Chevy Tahoe just as Nick was turning into the driveway. The Tahoe was going slow and Nick was immediately suspicious. When they got to the cabin, he went immediately and armed the women with 9mm pistols. For himself, he got his Kel-Tek 12-gauge pump loaded with 14 rounds of 3-inch magnum double-0 buckshot. He was already carrying his Glock 19.

"You all saw the black Tahoe that was crawlin' by when we got home," Nick said after he armed each of the women and verified they knew how to safely handle their weapon.

"We're being surveilled. They've found us. It's time to circle the wagons. They may hit us tonight."

"Did you call the sheriff's department?" Walela asked.

"I did. Unfortunately, we have no evidence that we're being targeted. They're aware of the events in Matamoros and Florida, but they want proof of harassment and cartel soldiers seen locally before they will begin an investigation. I reached out to the Texas Rangers and talked to Seth Buxton. He told me to alert him immediately and he will send help."

"Well that's comforting anyway," she replied.

"Judging from what I've seen so far," Nick observed, "They're tryin' to make us sweat. They want us to know they're coming. That's not the best tactic by any means. This is obviously for revenge and they don't mind sacrificing soldiers just to wage psychological warfare. At the same time, if they delay too long, there's the chance that we might get help."

"I just talked to mom," Walela announced. "They saw a black Tahoe near the house, but they started target practicing and it left."

"I want you all down in the cellar," Nick ordered. "Leave the door open so Ratchet can come and go. He'll alert you if anyone comes near the cabin. If he starts barkin', call him into the cellar and secure the door. Remember, this cabin has an automatic fire suppression system. If the fire alarm is triggered, the suppression system will fire in 15 seconds. It will remove all of the air on the ground floor and the attic by replacing it with CO_2. The system automatically dials 911, so just wait for the first responders to find you. By then, anyone still in the cabin will be dead from suffocation. The basement is an airtight storm shelter, so you should be okay. If the cabin should catch fire and the cellar starts to heat up, you can escape through the tunnel to the barn. I'll be outside. I'll take care of any threats out there. If you hear shooting, do not come out of the basement or the tunnel unless I tell you to open the door."

******

Earlier that day, a black Chevy Tahoe pulled up and parked near the Bell's home. One of the occupants began watching with binoculars. One of the four brothers spotted the Tahoe and alerted everyone. They had a quick discussion, bouncing ideas about what to do next.

Suddenly, Danuwoa said, "Why don't we put on a display for them?"

"What do you mean?" Aiyana asked.

"Remember when we used to have shooting competitions?"

"Yeah," One of the boys replied. "And Tala always got the highest score."

"Well, since she's not here," His older brother said, "Maybe you have a chance now!"

"Seriously," Danuwoa continued, "You all brought your rifles. Let's have a shooting competition right now. A special treat just for our uninvited guests."

The thug with the binoculars suddenly spoke up, "You're not gonna believe what they're doing."

"What?"

He handed the binoculars to one of the other two and said, "Check it out."

The second thug looked and said, "Damn! Looks like they're about to go to war. I see rifles everywhere."

"Look beyond where they're standing dipshit. What do you see?"

"Looks like six silhouette shooting targets."

"That's exactly what it is. They're about to start target practice."

"Yeah, I see. There's six of 'em. And they all have hunting rifles. With scopes."

Then the third thug spoke up, "That's two to one, man. I don't like them odds."

Just then all six of the Bell family began shooting at the targets at once.

"This is bullshit man." The third thug announced, "I ain't gettin' in no shooting war with a bunch of Cherokee Indians with deer rifles. They're excellent hunters and they shoot to kill. We're getting' the hell outta here!"

Danuwoa called for a cease fire and pointed to where the black Tahoe had been sitting. "Look!"

The only thing left of the Tahoe was a trail of dust.

******

After Bart Gris was advised by his crew in Balmorhea that they had found Nick Conner, his wife, her sister and another female, he immediately called his pilot and told him to get his jet ready to fly to Fort Stockton.

Gris had initially ordered Mateo to find and kill everyone involved with the murder of his man, Alphonze. Then he changed his orders. He not only wanted them to suffer, he decided that he would take charge of their torture before he personally killed them. And he wanted the sister for himself. Since they had been found at their cabin, he ordered his pilot to have a helicopter waiting when he landed at Fort Stockton. And just to be certain that there would be no problems, he was taking six of his men, including Pedro, his driver and bodyguard, with him, all well-armed, to back up the three men already on site.

Gris had also contacted Block and ordered him to find the architectural plans for the cabin and barn that were archived by the county planning and zoning along with the building permits.

******

Nick made certain the cellar door was secured, locked the cabin and headed for the pond. He submerged himself and waited. The late afternoon light was fading. Nick turned on the night vision scope on his Kel-Tek shotgun and began scanning for the bad guys.

He didn't have to wait long. His night scope began picking up movement in the distance. He saw three hostiles slowly moving toward the cabin. They spread out, and two of the hostiles disappeared as the cabin blocked Nick's view. He continued to track the hostile that he could see. The man stopped and crouched behind some cover, and then ran to the back door and attempted to kick it in. Nick aimed and fired. The man dropped to the ground.

Suddenly one of the other hostiles began firing an automatic weapon from the front of the cabin in Nick's general direction. Then he stopped firing, so Nick waited to see if he would move closer. Nick could hear banging and felt certain the third hostile was trying to break down the front door. He slowly crawled out of the pond and moved to get a better firing position. The hostile spotted Nick and began firing again, the bullets raking across the ground just in front of him. He quickly rolled further away from the line of fire, took aim and fired. The hostile fell backwards onto the front porch.

Then Nick heard a helicopter approaching and hoped that the Texas Rangers were finally arriving. The helicopter was running dark, with no marker lights on. Nick looked through his scope but was unable to identify the aircraft markings.

"I have a bad feelin' that ain't the cavalry." He thought.

Then the landing light illuminated and the helicopter dropped from sight toward a clearing near the highway not far from the cabin.

Nick watched and waited. Very shortly he saw the remaining one of the three hostiles moving fast in the direction of the helicopter. Moments later, multiple targets appeared in his night scope, moving toward the cabin. Since it appeared that the hostile didn't encounter any resistance, and Nick hadn't heard any law enforcement personnel identifying themselves, he knew the new arrivals were more bad guys.

Several of the hostiles began moving in his direction, so Nick slipped back into the pond. He swam underwater to an outcropping of rocks along the shore and carefully surveyed the area with his scope. Four hostiles were slowly moving in his direction. They were all wearing night vision goggles. Nick figured the cold water had given him an advantage by lowering his body temperature. He could take two of them out now, but the other two could easily pin him down before he could get to the bottom of the pond and out of range of the gunfire. So, Nick slipped back underwater and headed for the opposite side of the pond where he could circle around and ambush the hostiles from better cover.

He reached the waterfall, and slowly emerged from the pond, then quickly made his way to the other side of the barn. From there, Nick scanned the area with his scope and saw that the four hostiles had made it to the edge of the pond and were slowly moving across the yard toward his location.

From toward the cabin, Nick could hear loud banging from inside and his heart sank. The intruders had breached the front door, found the cellar door and were trying to break in. He wanted desperately to stop them from getting through the cellar door, but he knew there was little chance to make it from the barn to the cabin through four gunmen.

So Nick trusted his training and focused on eliminating as many of the immediate threats as possible. He waited until they were in range, targeted the two closest hostiles and opened fire. His first two shots brought both of the hostiles down. Instantly, the other two opened up with automatic weapons zeroed in on his location. Bullets ripped along the barn wall and ground around him. Nick rolled to get out of the line of fire but before he was clear a bullet ripped through his right arm just below his shoulder. He aimed and fired again, but the third hostile ran toward the fence, jumped it and headed across the pasture, out of range.

The hostile's intention was to cross the pasture and come around the barn from the corral and get behind Nick. Then he came to another fence and crossed it. He was about halfway across the pasture when he heard a rumbling sound. The hostile turned around just in time to see Attitude, head down, and charging full speed. Just as Attitude was about to hit him, the bull turned his head slightly and caught the hostile in the stomach with one of his horns, skewering the poor guy through and through. He screamed, but Attitude kept running as he approached the corral. Then, in one fluid motion, Attitude stopped and slung his head to the side, sending the doomed man flying through the air, and over the corral where he hit the ground near the barn with a loud thud. Nick quickly glanced toward the noise, saw the crumpled body of the hostile and said, "Thanks, Attitude."

Suddenly Pedro, the forth hostile, broke off his attack and headed for the cabin. Nick followed in hot pursuit. Just as Nick made it to the cabin, he realized that they had breached the cellar door and were already in the cellar. He could hear gunfire coming from the cellar and someone yelling, "Don't kill the young one!"

Walela had shot and killed the first intruder that came down the cellar stairs, but when they realized there were more coming, Walela sent Sprocket down the tunnel toward the barn and then they all followed him, firing at the intruders as they went.

Gris already knew about the tunnel from the drawings that Block uploaded to his phone. While he and one of his men waited in the cabin at the tunnel entrance, he ordered Pedro and the other man to go to the barn and wait for the women to come out on the other end of the tunnel. They went around to the opposite side of the house to avoid Nick, headed to the barn and was waiting at the tunnel exit.

The man turned to Pedro and said, "Gris said 'Don't kill the young one,' right?"

"That was his order," Pedro confirmed.

"Ok. Her sister killed Jack in the cellar. I'm takin' that bitch out when she comes out of the tunnel."

"Why kill her?" Pedro asked. "She's hot. The boss wants the young one, we can have some fun with her sister."

"There's plenty more hot women that didn't kill Jack. I'm takin' her out."

He stood near the tunnel exit and waited, expecting the women to emerge. Instead, Sprocket came out, saw the gun and attacked. He sunk his teeth into the man's gun arm with crushing force. The man yelled and fired his weapon, spraying bullets randomly. Pedro dove to avoid being shot.

Walela heard Sprocket attack, emerged first and shot and killed the man that Sprocket was attacking. Pedro jumped up, wrestled the gun from her and held her with his weapon pointed at her head. Sprocket growled and was about to attack. Pedro started to aim when Walela commanded Sprocket to stop.

"Smart dog," Pedro commented.

Just then Tala emerged, saw her sister's plight, and dropped her weapon.

"Call the other one to toss her gun up and come on out." Pedro ordered.

Tala called to Noya, she complied and emerged from the tunnel.

When Gris and the man with him saw Nick approaching the cabin, they both opened fire. Nick returned fire and they both went into the tunnel. He realized that following them into the tunnel was likely a trap, so he slowly moved toward the barn. He saw Pedro holding the gun on Walela. Just then Gris and the thug with him emerged from the tunnel and Nick realized it was too risky to try anything there, so he ran toward the helicopter, intending to ambush the pilot, but he was on guard and saw Nick coming.

He opened fire, forcing Nick to take cover. When Gris, his men and the women arrived at the helicopter, Gris and Pedro forced the three women into the helicopter while the other man fired at Nick, keeping him pinned while the pilot spooled up the helicopter. When the thug stopped firing in order to board the chopper, Nick fired once and he fell to the ground.

Gris and Pedro began firing at Nick. Noya took advantage of the situation, jumped from the helicopter and ran. Pedro pointed his weapon at Noya, but Gris said, "To Hell with her. I've got what I want. Go! Go!"

The pilot lifted off and headed for the jet parked at Fort Stockton airport. Gris called his pilot and ordered him to spool up the jet and be ready for takeoff as soon as they boarded. Nick watched as the helicopter climbed and turned east, returning in the direction that it came.

Chapter 18 The Chase

After Noya escaped from the helicopter, she ran toward the cabin and then spotted Nick, so she took cover behind him.

"Are you okay?" He asked.

"No, I'm pissed," Noya replied, "Now they have Tala *and* Walela."

"Not for long if I have anything to say about it. Come on."

Nick started running toward the cabin.

"Where are we going?" She asked as she tried to keep up.

"To get my Durango."

"Then what?"

"We're gonna catch that helicopter."

"We're gonna what?"

When they got to the Durango, Nick jumped in and hit the start button, hoping that the key fob still worked considering it had been in his pocket while he was in the pond.

The powerful hemi roared to life just as Noya climbed in.

"Buckle up," Nick ordered, and hit the accelerator.

The Hellcat screamed as the supercharger spooled up and lurched forward, throwing gravel and dirt as it accelerated down the driveway.

Noya tried to hold on as she exclaimed, "Holy crap!"

Nick steered the Hellcat right when he got to FM 3078. The paved road provided better traction than the gravel road, but still he had to fight the steering wheel to keep it straight due to the tires losing traction as it rocketed forward, pinning them in their seats.

"Where are you going?" Noya asked. "Didn't the helicopter go the other way?"

"We'd have to slow down to go through Balmorhea or risk havin' a wreck. I don't plan on slowin' down."

"Oh my," Noya moaned.

When they reached the eastbound on-ramp to Interstate-10, Nick slowed just enough to keep the machine under control getting to the blacktop and then opened it up. Noya was pinned to the seat by the G-force as she watched the speedometer quickly pass 160 MPH.

"On my God!" She exclaimed.

The Hellcat topped out holding around 178 MPH. Nick was passing semi-trucks and cars like they were standing still, on the left, the right, or the emergency lanes, whatever was available.

"Look for the helicopter ahead of us," Nick said, "We should be catchin' up. They're probably runnin' dark, but we should be able to pick him out against the lighter backdrop of the sky."

"We're going so fast, we might be outrunning the speed of light!" Noya replied frantically.

Then Nick said, "I hope I'm not wrong about where they're goin'. They came from the east, and Fort Stockton is the closest public airport. Do you still have your cellphone or did they take it?"

"I have it. I guess in all the bedlam they forgot to take our phones."

"Call the Fort Stockton airport. Hopefully the FBO is still open."

"FBO?"

"The Fixed Base Operator. They provide fuel services and the like."

"Oh, okay."

Noya searched and found the number, dialed it and handed the phone to Nick.

"Put it on speaker," Nick requested.

Suddenly Noya noticed blood dripping from Nick's right elbow and yelled, "You've been shot!"

"Yeah, I couldn't help but notice."

Noya ripped a strip of cloth from Nick's shirttail and tied it around his arm in an attempt to reduce his blood loss.

As she tightened the makeshift bandage, Nick yelled "Oww!"

"Sorry!" Noya replied.

"You're doin' great, thanks," Nick reassured her.

"Who am I speakin' to?" Nick asked.

"This is Frank, at Fort Stockton-Pecos County Airport, I'm the fuel specialist."

"Okay Frank, I'm Nick. I'm eastbound on I-10, heading your way. There's a helicopter that I think is inbound from Balmorhea. There are two kidnapped women on board. Will you please call the Texas Rangers, Waco Company F. Ask to speak with Lieutenant Seth Buxton. Tell him that Nick Conner needs his help ASAP at your location. You got that?"

"Why don't you just call him yourself?"

"I follow your logic Frank, but I need you on this call. You have a serious crime about to go down there, and I need your help. Please put me on hold, make the call and then punch me in."

Several minutes later Frank came on the line. *"Standby Nick, I'm conferencing you in. Okay Nick, Lieutenant Buxton is on the line"*

"Thanks Frank. Lieutenant, this is Nick Conner. We also have Frank with Fort Stockton Airport on with us. The cartel dropped the hammer. They have taken Walela and Tala.

"Frank, is an executive jet spooling up on your ramp right now?"

"Yes. I just refueled it. But how did you know that?"

"Just a lucky guess. I think that jet brought members of the California Cartel here. They flew from there to Balmorhea on a helicopter, kidnapped my wife and her sister and now they're headed back to Fort Stockton. The jet is waiting to take them back to California. I'm on I-10, tryin' to catch up to the helicopter now. Seth, can you provide support?"

"We have two mobile units in Van Horn. I'll alert them. I'll also get every DPS unit in the area in route immediately."

"I appreciate it Seth. Just please let the responders know that three hostiles, including the pilot, is onboard, and they are well armed. They have two hostages, my wife, Walela, and her sister, Tala. We should be at the airport shortly. Do not let that jet takeoff!"

Buxton hung up and said, "Damn it! They've kidnapped Tala again and have her sister, too!"

Frank hung up, then ran to his fuel truck, drove it on the ramp, and parked it in front of the jet. Then he took the keys, stuck his knife into the sidewall of the left front tire, and ran. The pilot came out on the passenger stairs and yelled at him to move the fuel truck, but Frank kept running.

All this time, Nick had been driving 175 MPH, trying to catch up to the helicopter. When he met a Texas State Trooper running radar from the westbound lanes, she immediately began pursuit, but had very little chance of catching up to Nick. She called and reported that she was in pursuit of a Dodge Durango traveling eastbound at extreme speeds. Then she received the radio message from the Texas Rangers about the kidnapping.

Suddenly, Noya spotted the helicopter.

"I see it!" she said, and pointed towards it.

"Looks like he's on approach to the airport. And he's turned on his marker lights. I guess he's not fond of midair collisions," Nick commented. "We should be there in a few minutes."

As Nick approached the security gate leading to the airport ramps and runways, it began to open.

"Way to go, Frank!" Nick said as he flew through the gate and turned the Hellcat towards the jet sitting on the ramp. Behind the jet, the helicopter had just touched down. Nick stopped at a safe distance, told Noya to keep down, then got out and dropped down behind the Hellcat, with a shooting vantage point so he could see the helicopter and the jet.

Gris was in a difficult position. The jet couldn't move and the helicopter didn't have enough range to provide a viable escape route.

Suddenly a Texas DPS Chevy Tahoe arrived, passed by Nick and stopped near to the helicopter. Pedro jumped out of the helicopter and started firing at the DPS vehicle. The officer jumped out, dropped down behind the driver's door and fired several shots. She hit Pedro, he fell, then tried to get back into the helicopter. She fired again and he went down.

Gris began firing an automatic weapon at the Trooper. Just then, Walela kicked the pilot in the face, then she and Tala jumped out of the opposite door and ran. The Trooper saw the girls running away and ran to help them.

Nick saw the girls running, opened Noya's door and told her to go help them. Then he jumped in the driver's seat and began moving toward the DPS vehicle. When Gris saw the Trooper running away and realized that the girls were gone, he headed for the DPS vehicle. When he was about to climb in the driver's seat, he saw Nick moving toward him and opened fire. The bullets raked across the front of the Hellcat, Nick ducked and steam gushed from the radiator.

Gris jumped in and roared away, heading for the airport gate. Nick fired at him as he passed, but missed. He watched as Gris exited the airport and turned onto Highway 285, the Texas Pecos Trail, heading northwest. Then Nick ran to the helicopter. The pilot was still reeling from being kicked in the face by Walela.

Nick looked at the pilot, "How much fuel remaining?"

"Enough for about a hundred miles, but I'm not flying you anywhere."

"I ain't askin' you to fly," Nick replied, then pointed his weapon at him and said, "Get out."

Just then the women, including the Trooper, came running to the helicopter. Walela kissed and hugged Nick, then Tala hugged him.

Walela saw the blood and yelled, "Nick! You've been shot!"

"It's okay, Noya took care of it."

Then Nick looked at the Trooper, "Thank you ma'am for your help."

"You're very welcome, sir. And you need first aid for that gunshot wound."

"Thanks, but I have to go huntin' right now."

Then he pointed at the pilot and said, "Please arrest this man for kidnappin', attempted murder, and assault with a deadly weapon. He shot at me."

Then he looked at the Trooper somewhat sheepishly, and added, "And, uh, I'm sorry about the speedin'…"

Then Nick walked over to Pedro's body, picked up the automatic weapon that he'd been using and checked the ammo level. He felt Pedro's pockets, found two full magazines and took them.

Then he looked at Tala, handed her the rifle and said, "Hey gunfighter, wanna go for a ride?"

"Where?" She asked as she looked at the rifle.

"Huntin' a DPS Tahoe with an asshole in it."

"What are we going to drive?" Tala asked.

"This," Nick replied, pointing at the helicopter.

"You can fly a helicopter?" Tala and Walela asked simultaneously.

"We'll find out in a minute," Nick replied as he climbed into the right seat.

They looked at each other in surprise, then Tala climbed in as the engine started and began spooling up.

"I'm going, too," Walela announced and climbed in after her.

"I'll just stay here," Noya said, then looked at the Trooper, "I've flown enough today."

"My Radar showed 175," The Trooper said.

"His speedometer did, too," Noya replied.

"Really? Huh," she said, and then looked at the Hellcat.

Nick handed his Glock to Walela as she climbed into the co-pilot's seat, then he lifted off in the direction that Gris had fled.

Very shortly several State Troopers arrived at the airport. And after that, two Texas Rangers Law Enforcement units. Then two Sheriff's Department units arrived. The Trooper updated everyone on the events. Border Patrol dispatched a helicopter from Van Horn and the Rangers dispatched a helicopter from Waco. Noya informed one of the Sheriff's Deputies that there were a bunch of dead guys waiting for them at the cabin in Balmorhea.

Nick leveled the helicopter out at 500 feet and pushed it to the maximum speed, watching for vehicle tail lights in the distance. There was just a faint glow of sunlight on the distant horizon, otherwise it was a dark, moonless night.

"We should be able to see his lights," Nick commented. "It's too dark to run without lights tonight. Especially, if he goes off road, he'd end up down in some arroyo."

Walela unbuckled, then searched and found the first aid kit and proceeded to dress Nick's wound.

"You have bled all over your right side. Do you have any other wounds?"

"I don't think so. This one hurts enough."

"I'm sorry," she said and kissed him on the cheek.

"You need to buckle up, things may get a bit rough when we catch him."

One by one they overtook vehicles headed toward Pecos on the Texas Pecos Trail. When they came to FM1776, Nick swung right heading north toward Coyanosa.

"It's not likely that he would head for Pecos," Nick speculated. "By now there'll be a BOLO for the stolen DPS vehicle. There's always a possibility that he's stopped to hide somewhere along the way, but I feel like he'll try to get as far into the boonies as he can, then coordinate with someone to meet him and dump the DPS rig."

"It does not help that he has access to a police radio," Walela said.

"That's for certain."

"What are we going to do when we find him?" Tala asked.

"Shoot him," Walela replied.

"Sound's good to me," Tala commented.

"Let's let him start shootin' first," Nick suggested. "Then we'll shoot him."

In the distance, the lights from Coyanosa could be seen, otherwise very few cars could be seen ahead. As they overflew Coyanosa, Tala saw people in a restaurant parking lot, walking toward the front door. They looked up to watch the helicopter fly by.

Nick looked down and said, "That pilot wasn't kiddin', we're gettin' low on gas."

"Can't we just stop at a gas station?" Tala asked.

"That would be nice, but even if we could, they don't carry our flavor. We need jet fuel."

"Oh well…" she replied as she sighed. "I'm not going to walk to the next airport."

Ahead, FM1776 jogged to the right and then continued on north toward Monahans - Thorntonville and Interstate 20. The interstate traffic formed a long, dotted line of lights moving along the horizon on either side of the small villages.

"We're in luck," Nick announced. "I see an airport beacon ahead."

Suddenly, just ahead, Walela spotted a vehicle traveling faster than the other traffic and pointed it out.

"Let's get a closer look at that vehicle right there."

"I see that," Nick replied. "Your wish is my command, my love."

He pushed the stick forward and the aircraft nosed over and descended. Nick eased the collective lever down and slowed the forward speed to match the vehicle. Then he switched on the landing light. The black and white DPS paint scheme lit up, as well as the number on the roof.

"Well, if it's not our guy, some Trooper is gonna be pissed."

Gris slammed on brakes, causing Nick to overfly him. Then he jumped out and began firing at them.

Nick made a hard 180 turn and positioned Tala in perfect firing position.

Then he said, "Okay Gunfighter, open your door. Get a good grip on that weapon. Remember, it is full auto and will try to jump out of your hands."

Tala opened the door, flipped the safety off, aimed and fired.

She stopped firing for a second, looked at the weapon and said, "Damn!"

Then she opened it up again. Bullets poured out of her rifle, peppering Gris and the vehicle. Gris fell to his knees but kept firing. Rounds could be heard hitting the fuselage.

Tala's rifle stopped firing as she emptied the magazine. She ejected the empty magazine, inserted the full spare, hit the button to jack a round into the chamber and readied to fire again as Nick circled once more to put her in a clear firing position.

She fired again, this time with deadly accuracy, ripping Gris to shreds. He was aiming to fire when the rifle flew out of his hands, sparks flying from it as the projectiles hit the steel receiver and barrel. When Tala stopped firing, Gris lay sprawled on the ground, his white silk shirt stained red with blood.

Nick hovered there a moment, watching to make sure Gris wasn't moving.

"Good shooting, Gunfighter!"

"Thanks," Tala replied, "It was a pleasure."

Then he turned and headed to Roy Hurd Memorial Airport for fuel and keyed the radio:

"Roy Hurd Unicom, this is helicopter 86 Tango, 20 miles out, inbound from the south, full stop for Jet-A."

"86 Tango, this is Roy Hurd, winds 220 at 8 knots, altimeter 29.78. No reported traffic. You're cleared to land. Fueler will be waiting."

"86 Tango roger. Thanks. See you in a bit."

In the distance toward the west, the flashing marker beacons of two helicopters could be seen heading toward their location.

After Nick refueled, they lifted off and headed back to Fort Stockton. In the distance, they could see law enforcement and emergency vehicle lights flashing, as well as the two helicopter marker beacons flashing.

Suddenly the radio came to life.

"86 Tango, this is Texas Rangers Air Unit 8. How do you read?"

"Unit 8, 86 Tango, you're loud and clear, go ahead."

"86 Tango, Unit 8, are you en route to Fort Stockton? And do you have any info on the individual responsible for the stolen Texas DPS vehicle?"

"Unit 8, 86 Tango, 'that's affirmative, we're returning to Fort Stockton. We pursued the stolen DPS vehicle after he left the airport. We finally caught up with him there at your location, but it appeared someone had been there before us. We didn't want to disturb the scene, and we were bingo for fuel, so we headed to Roy Hurd for some Jet-A."

"86 Tango, Unit 8, how did you know the individual was a 'he'?"

"Unit 8, 86 Tango, well, he was shootin' at us right before he stole the DPS vehicle. That's why we were tryin' to catch up to him."

Long silence.

(The Texas Ranger talking to Nick on the radio turned to this partner and said, "That bastard knows who killed this jerk. I know it.")

"Copy 86 Tango, Unit 8, have a safe flight."

"You as well. 86 Tango."

Nick turned, looked at Tala and winked.

She just smiled.

On their return flight, just after they flew past Grandfalls, Nick flew over the Imperial Reservoir, a 1500 acre lake just south of the Pecos River. Without saying a word, Nick set the autopilot to hover mode over the middle of the lake, got out of the pilot's seat and then sat down beside Tala.

Walela looked at the controls and then looked at Nick and said, "Oh my God! You could have said something!"

He winked at Tala, then looked at Walela and replied, "Then it wouldn't have been a surprise."

She gave him a very mean look in return and said, "Someone needs to whip your ass!

If you weren't wounded…"

Nick picked up the rifle that Tala had used and began to disassemble it. He opened both of the doors and pitched the pieces out one door and then the other until all of the pieces were gone.

Then he closed the doors, looked at Tala and said, "What rifle?"

She just smiled again and hugged him.

Chapter 19 And So…

When Nick landed the helicopter at Fort Stockton Airport, they were met by Lieutenant Buxton of the Texas Rangers.

Nick stepped out on the ramp, shook his hand and said, "Howdy Lieutenant, I really appreciate your help during all of this."

"I'm glad that I was able to help, Nick, and very pleased that Walela and Tala are safe."

As he said that, he was looking at Tala. She looked back at him curiously.

Walela took Tala's hand, walked to where Nick and the lieutenant were standing and said, "Tala, this is Lieutenant Seth Buxton of the Texas Rangers. He was the first man to offer to help me find you. And he has never forgotten you, and never given up trying to find you. Lieutenant, this is my sister, Tala."

Lt. Buxton started to reach out and shake Tala's hand, but she grabbed him and hugged him tightly.

He smiled and said, "That is the best hug I think I have ever received."

Then he took her shoulders, looked into her eyes and said, "I am so happy to meet you Tala. I've been looking forward to this day since my first meeting with your sister. She has fought very hard to get you back home."

"I know, sir," Tala replied. "I'm so blessed to have you, my sister, Nick, and my family in my life. I'm thankful to so many."

"Young lady, it was our job – the job of all of us – to find you and get you back home safe. I'm thankful that I was able to play a small part in that successful effort."

"Lieutenant, you are an honorable man."

"Thank you…" Then he smiled and said, "Tala, if I were younger…"

Tala smiled and kissed him on the cheek.

Just then, two well-dressed men started to walk toward them.

The Lieutenant turned to Nick. "I met you when you landed to tell you that two US Marshals are here to question you about how Gris died."

The two men walked up to Nick.

"Mr. Conner, I'm US Marshal Simmons and this is US Marshal Blake. We're part of the National Human Trafficking Victim Recovery Team."

Both displayed their badge.

Blake spoke next. "Mr. Conner, we understand that you, your wife and Miss Bell pursued Mr. Gris in a helicopter as he fled the airport earlier tonight. Is that correct?"

"Yes, that is correct," Nick replied.

"Mr. Gris was found shot to death a short time later, on FM1776, south of Roy Hurd Airport where you landed to refuel before you returned to Fort Stockton Airport. When questioned, you stated via the aircraft radio that you had no knowledge of how Mr. Gris came to be killed. Is that correct?"

"Yes, that is correct."

"By all accounts, your aircraft was the only one seen in the area before federal and state authorities arrived on scene. How do you explain that?"

"As I stated on the radio, we saw that he was apparently dead. I chose not to land and contaminate the crime scene. We needed fuel, so I landed at Roy Hurd Airport."

"According to investigators, Mr. Gris was hit with approximately thirty rounds of .223 ammo, and it appeared that the shots came from above the victim."

"I'd hardly call Gris a victim, but I can't say that another aircraft wasn't at that location before we arrived. If some pilot chooses to run dark on a night like this, his aircraft won't be seen. It's that simple. That's how the drug runners do it."

"What type of weapons were you carrying onboard your helicopter?"

"I had my Glock, and that was it."

"How did you propose to stop Gris from fleeing with just one sidearm?"

"I didn't. I just hoped to find him and then report his position to the authorities."

"Why did you take your wife and her sister with you?"

"They volunteered, and I needed their sharp eyes, especially considering that it is a dark, moonless night."

At that point, someone handed Marshall Blake an empty .223 shell casing and told him that it had been found inside the helicopter that Nick had just landed.

"Mr. Conner, this shell casing was found inside the aircraft that you just landed. How do you explain that?"

"Well, Marshall Blake, to be completely honest, I actually stole that helicopter from Gris. He and his thugs flew it to my cabin earlier today, and tried to kill me, and then kidnapped my wife and her sister. When they landed here, I was waiting, and shortly, a State Trooper arrived. Gris and his thugs started shooting automatic weapons at us from inside the helicopter. I'm sure that's where that shell casing came from. You can check the bullet holes in my Hellcat and the DPS Tahoe that Gris stole. Those bullet holes were made by .223 automatic weapons fire. After Gris fled, I stole the helicopter and used it to pursue him."

Blake looked at Simmons and sighed.

"Well, I think that answers our questions sufficiently. Mr. Conner, thank you for your cooperation."

"Any time, Marshall Blake."

Then Simmons turned to Nick and said, "Is that really your Hellcat?"

"Yes it is," Nick replied.

"With the supercharger?"

"Yep. 710 horses."

"Oh wow, I'll bet that thing will fly."

"If it had wings…" Nick replied smiling.

Noya was listening and butted in, "Yea, it almost flew tonight with me in it!"

"They told me that Gris shot it. I'm sorry," Simmons said as he looked at the bullet holes in the hood and grill.

"No serious damage done I hope. I think it just needs a hood, grill and a radiator," Nick replied.

Then Marshall Blake looked back, saw Simmons talking to Nick and yelled, "Simmons! Let's get the hell out of here!"

Simmons shook Nick's hand and said, "Take it easy," and headed towards Blake.

Three weeks later, a crime scene cleaning crew had completed a thorough sweep and repair of the cabin and grounds. Everything was restored, just as it was. The older couple that owned the place found a home in Italy and decided to live there, so they offered the cabin for sale. Nick bought it for cash and then he and Walela hired a local couple to oversee the cabin, livestock and property on a long-term basis. Then they loaded up Sprocket and headed for Muscogee.

A few days after they arrived, Nick asked Walela to go for a walk with him.

"Hummingbird, I have a confession. You're not the only one that has not been truthful."

"Does it have to do with one of your old girlfriends in Destin?"

Nick hesitated, then replied, "No, this is just about me. I haven't been honest with you."

"What do you mean?"

"When I told you that my retirement portfolio is valued at two million dollars, I wasn't being honest."

"That's okay. We can get by. We're doing great so far, right?"

"No, you don't understand. You see, when my dad was a kid, my granddad owned a pretty big ranch north of San Angelo. And he was a very successful rancher. Dad, his brothers and sisters all worked on the ranch, but dad was interested in other things.

"One day, when he was about eight, he was waiting in the dentist office and picked up a copy of the Wall Street Journal. He started reading and was completely captivated by the articles. He asked the dentist if he could take it home. The dentist said 'yes' and he almost wore the paper out, reading it over and over.

"So grandad and grandma got dad a subscription. He still maintains that same subscription to this very day. He is obsessed with numbers and finance. That's why he became an investment banker with the oil industry. He was a millionaire by age nineteen and paid for his own education at Harvard Business School, where he earned a doctorate in Business Administration. His hobby is numbers and finance. Business is all he ever thinks about. I've never seen him go fishin' or huntin'.

"Don't get me wrong, he likes the outdoors. He's an excellent horseman and wrangler. He also has some of the best quarter horses and thoroughbred race horses in Texas. He typically runs about 5000 head of cattle, mostly premium beef cattle."

"So, what are you saying, Nick? Are you planning on going into ranching?"

"Sweetheart, I had a great career in the SEALS. That was my chosen path and my parents were behind me all the way. But all that ended. Since then, I've been an entitled jerk. I became a civil engineer. I did manage some pretty large projects for BLM. I just wanted to prove that I was capable of being a productive member of society even though I have a brain injury. But I didn't need the money. I donated all of my salary to charity."

"I don't understand." Walela said. "Why didn't you need the money?"

"I'm a full partner with my dad in our company called, Conner Ranch LLC."

"So?"

"Hummingbird, our ranch is 16,000 acres. We have over a hundred oil wells. We have timber, sawmills, horses, cattle, sheep, lamas, emus, pigs, and chickens. We grow cotton, corn, soybeans, wheat, barley. We have our own runway. Dad has three planes, I have two, and we have two helicopters, all in our own hangars. Dad has a collection of classic cars. I have a dozen high performance cars and trucks. Our net worth is over 200 million dollars."

Walela's mouth dropped open and she just stared at him wide-eyed. Nick reached out, closed her mouth, looked into her wide eyes and very slowly said, "Two… hundred… million… dollars."

Walela slowly replied, "Oh… my… God!"

After getting over the initial shock, and having a long discussion with Nick about the future, Walela came back to earth and began to get some perspective on how her life was about to change. They discussed everything with her parents. Nick paid off all of the family's mortgages and loans. He also bought everyone a new vehicle of their choice. Tala chose a black Ford Bronco Raptor. Nick hired Noya to manage the computer systems for the entire Conner ranch at a salary twenty percent higher than her salary with Shephard Center.

After several weeks at the Bell's home, Nick and Walela were officially married (she proposed to him). It was a formal outdoor wedding at her home just the way she wanted, with a Cherokee Baptist Minister.

Nick's buddy, Tim, flew his wife, Julie, along with Nick's buddies, Jack (F-22 pilot) and his wife, Allie, and Dave (F-35 pilot) and his wife, Susan, to Oklahoma for the wedding in one of Nick's planes, a Pilatus PC-12 NGX luxury single engine turboprop.

Nick's dad and mom flew to the wedding in his dad's Piaggio Aerospace Avanti P180 Evo luxury business turboprop. For their honeymoon gift, Nick's dad provided his plane and a pilot to fly Nick and Walela to Nassau. While there, they rented a sailboat and sailed around the Bahamas for two months. Walela's baby bump was beginning to show quite a bit by then, so they flew back to Muscogee.

Before the wedding, Nick had called his former commander with the SEALS, told him Tala's story and explained that he wanted to present the SEAL Trident Pin to her as an award for the bravery she had shown during their escape from Mexico. His commander contacted the base commander and they decided to go one further.

Nick flew the Bell and Connor families to San Diego, where, on-board Naval Amphibious Base (NAB), Coronado, at an assembly at the Naval Special Warfare Command Headquarters, with all present, Commander, NAB Coronado, officiated over a special awards ceremony:

"Ladies and gentlemen, it is my pleasure and privilege to present the following awards with citation."

Ten-hut!

"On or about the night of March 10th 2024, in the face of withering automatic gun fire from combatants in a pursuing vehicle, Miss Tala Bell, wielding a single sidearm, did take out two of the attacking combatants, and successfully defended herself, ten of her fellow human trafficking kidnap victims, and the driver of the rickety and run-down Chevy van in which they were fleeing, former Navy SEAL, Lt. Commander Nick Conner.

"Miss Bell, I am honored to award you the US Navy Superior Civilian Award for Valor Medal, and the coveted SEAL Trident Pin. You are now an honorary Navy SEAL. Young lady, you humble this old warrior. You are a true hero and you bring honor to us all."

Tala accepted the medal and pin with a big smile amidst thunderous applause and then hugged the Captain.

After another week at the Bell's in Muscogee, Nick, Walela, Tala and Sprocket flew to Destin. Nick shipped his repaired Hellcat, Walela's F-150 Raptor and Tala's Bronco Raptor to Destin so they would each have transportation when they arrived.

Walela had never seen Destin, and since it was going to be their Florida home, Nick wanted her to decorate her home as she pleased and make it hers.

Walela and Tala enjoyed the boat and especially going to Crab Island. Tala fell in love with Blue Water Runner and decided to get her US Coast Guard captain's license so she could run the boat herself. She also wanted to learn to fly Nick's plane. Since Nick's buddy, Tim, was a Certified Flight Instructor, he started giving her flying lessons. It would be an extended process to become qualified to fly the Pilatus, but Tala was determined.

Sprocket absolutely loved the beach and riding on the boat. He became one of the family with Nick's buddies and stayed at their houses almost as much as he stayed at home.

As the weeks flew by and the time for the baby's arrival grew closer, Nick flew Walela home more often to spend time with her mom. She decided to have the baby at her mom's with the aid of a Cherokee midwife.

On a cool, crisp morning in October, Walela gave birth to a beautiful, healthy 8 pound, 10 ounce boy. They named him Waya Nickolas Conner. Waya in Cherokee means Wolf. Tala was delighted.

As Walela held her newborn son, she looked at Nick sitting beside her, kissed him on the cheek, and then she looked at her son, smiled and said, "Grandmother would be pleased…"

The End